YOURS FOREVER

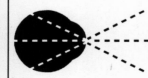 This Large Print Book carries the
Seal of Approval of N.A.V.H.

YOURS FOREVER

FARRAH ROCHON

THORNDIKE PRESS
A part of Gale, Cengage Learning

GALE
CENGAGE Learning·

Farmington Hills, Mich • San Francisco • New York • Waterville, Maine
Meriden, Conn • Mason, Ohio • Chicago

GALE
CENGAGE Learning·

Copyright © 2014 by Farrah Roybiskie.
Bayou Dreams Series #2.
Thorndike Press, a part of Gale, Cengage Learning.

LIBRARY OF CONGRESS CATALOGING-IN-PUBLICATION DATA

Rochon, Farrah.
   Yours forever / by Farrah Rochon. — Large print edition.
      pages ; cm. — (Thorndike Press large print African-American) (Bayou dreams series ; #2)
   ISBN 978-1-4104-6951-9 (hardcover) — ISBN 1-4104-6951-4 (hardcover)
   1. African Americans—Fiction. 2. Family secrets—Fiction. 3. Louisiana—Fiction. 4. Large type books. I. Title.
PS3618.O346Y68 2014
813'.6—dc23   2014005147

Published in 2014 by arrangement with Harlequin Books S.A.

Printed in Mexico
1 2 3 4 5 6 7 18 17 16 15 14

Dear Reader,

I don't know about you, but I'm fascinated by the study of genealogy. Maybe it's because I come from a large family. Those old stories that were staples around the dinner table piqued my inquisitive mind as a young girl, and I've always wanted to dig into my family's history.

One of the coolest things about the internet is the ease with which a person can now study their family's past. With the click of a mouse you can discover a plethora of interesting facts about your ancestors. For Professor Tamryn West, the heroine of *Yours Forever,* researching her great-great-grandmother's past is more than just something cool to do on the internet; it is her life's passion.

I hope you enjoy following Tamryn on her journey as she uncovers the secrets of her family's past . . . and finds love in the place she least expects.

I thank you for returning to the town of Gauthier, Louisiana, with me. Come back next month for another story in the Bayou Dreams series, *Forever's Promise.* I am positive that you will fall in love with Shayla and Xavier.

Happy reading,
Farrah Rochon

For my traveling buddy, my aunt,
Catherine Gray.
Looking forward to many more
adventures!

But as for you, be strong and do not give up, for your work will be rewarded.

— *2 Chronicles* 15:6–8

CHAPTER 1

"How did I end up here?"

Tamryn West stumbled over a clump of dried mud as she walked along the dirt-and-gravel road. She did her best Statue of Liberty impersonation as she pointed her cell phone skyward and tried to find a signal. Shielding her eyes against the sun's rays, she spun in a slow circle, hoping to spot something other than the trees and high weeds that seemed to stretch for miles all around her.

"How in the *hell* did I end up here?"

And who would she have to murder at the car-rental company for renting her a car with a busted radiator? She was no automobile expert, but after eight years in Boston she'd refilled the antifreeze enough times to know how a radiator should look, and it should definitely not have steam blowing out of it like a pot of boiling pasta.

She held the phone up to the sky again,

but got the same result. Zero bars. Was it really a surprise that the Middle of Nowhere, Louisiana, wouldn't have cell-phone service?

Tamryn peered down the road she'd been traveling, trying to recall the last house she'd passed. It had been at least five miles back. Possibly more.

She was *not* walking for miles in these heels. She'd probably have better luck if she continued traveling east instead of backtracking. According to her cell phone's GPS — back when it was working and before it started recalculating over and over again — she had been only fifteen miles from the town of Gauthier.

That meant she should only have about five miles or so to go, right?

Of course, that was before her ill-advised detour onto this dirt road.

"No use beating yourself up over it," Tamryn told herself, blowing out a weary breath.

The best thing she could do right now was get moving. She'd been out here for nearly an hour already, and not a single car had passed. She would have to walk until she found some sign of life, or at least enough bars on her cell phone to send an SOS text message.

Tamryn started back for the rental car to

12

retrieve her laptop, because even though there had been no sign of life on this road, she would not chance having her laptop stolen. All of her important files were backed up on several flash drives, but that didn't matter. She wouldn't be able to make it a day without her computer.

The rumble of an engine broke into the stillness that had surrounded her for the past hour. Tamryn surveyed the area ahead and spotted a cloud of red dust mushrooming in the distance. A shiny motorcycle appeared, emerging from the cloud like a ghost come to life.

Her heart rate escalated.

This could be a good thing, or it could be a very, *very* bad thing.

She was a woman alone on a back road in an unfamiliar town. She had no cell-phone service, and even in a pair of Nikes she could only manage a comfortable jog. If she had to outrun some unsavory character on a motorcycle while wearing these heels, she'd just as well give up right now.

"Enough with the dramatics," Tamryn said. Maybe Motorcycle Guy was a perfectly safe gentleman taking a leisurely Sunday-afternoon bike ride around the countryside. For all she knew, he could be a seventy-year-old retiree trying to recapture his youth.

Motorcycle Guy started to let off the gas about ten yards ahead of her, so that by the time he reached the tail end of her rental car, his bike kicked up only a smattering of dust.

He stopped and steadied his legs on the ground, and one thing became immediately clear: this was no seventy-year-old retiree, not with the way his solid black T-shirt hugged his leanly muscled biceps, shoulders and chest. It was obvious his jeans had seen better days, but the way the worn fabric molded to his legs literally made her mouth water. He wore dark sunglasses, nearly as black as his gleaming motorcycle helmet.

Well, if she had to play the damsel in distress, at least her knight in shining armor was smoking-hot.

"Car trouble?" he asked in a deep, smooth voice.

Tamryn nodded. "It's the radiator."

"That's never good." He dropped the kickstand into place and climbed off the massive black-and-chrome motorcycle, removing his helmet and hanging it on the handlebar. Tamryn studied his easy gait as he made his way to the front where she'd left the hood up. He braced his hands against the compact car's frame and leaned over, studying the engine.

She thought the jeans had molded magnificently to his legs, but that was nothing compared to how the denim cupped his ass. Sheer perfection.

"It doesn't look good," he said, backing from underneath the hood. He dusted his hands off on his backside. "You'll need to call a tow truck."

Tamryn held her phone up to him. "That would be a lot easier if there was cell-phone service."

A corner of his mouth curled up, and her heart did a two-step. Who would have thought such a small smile could do *that* much for a man's face.

"Are you heading to Gauthier?" he asked.

"Yes, I'm staying at a bed-and-breakfast called Belle Mansion."

"Belle Maison," he corrected her.

"Ah, yes. Forgive my rusty French," she said. "I forgot for a minute that I was in Louisiana."

And there was that smile again. The man had dimples. Extremely cute, extremely sexy dimples.

"You're only a few miles from Belle Maison." He gestured toward his bike. "Hop on. I'll give you a ride into town and send a tow truck out to get the car." He held his hand out to her. "I'm Matt, by the way."

"Tamryn," she answered, shaking his hand, which was much smoother than she'd anticipated. It went against his rough-and-tough biker image. Although, as she got a closer look at him, she acknowledged that he didn't seem all that rough. His light brown skin was practically flawless, his haircut close and trimmed with precision. Tamryn glanced at his hands. The nails were neat, without a speck of dirt underneath them.

Her eyes returned to his face and she noticed there was something extremely familiar about him.

"Do you want a ride?" he asked.

"Uh . . . what?" She shook her head to clear it.

He pulled his sunshades down and peered at her over the rim. His brows lifted, and he hooked a thumb toward the bike. "A ride? To Belle Maison?"

Tamryn reared back with a start.

It was *him.* Matthew Gauthier. The man who had been avoiding every effort she'd made to contact him over the past six months.

Dressed in jeans and a T-shirt, he looked nothing like the impeccably attired attorney she'd spotted in the few photos she'd been able to find of him during her numerous

16

Google searches.

"You can wait with the car, but I don't recommend it," he continued. "Once that sun starts setting it won't be long before it's pitch-black out here. I'd much rather take you with me."

There was something about the way his voice dropped on that last statement that made her spine tingle with all sorts of . . . interesting sensations.

No. No, no, no. This was a spine-tingling-free trip. She was in Louisiana for a specific purpose, and it had nothing to do with indulging in tingles of any kind, especially those brought on by cute dimples and well-fitting jeans.

She'd allowed herself to be distracted from completing her research before and, courtesy of her best friend and colleague, Victoria Brown, had an *I Played the Fool* T-shirt to prove it. She'd even brought the T-shirt down here with her as a reminder of what she would not be doing again.

The unwelcome reminder of her previous lapse in judgment quickly squelched the stubborn remaining tingles and brought her focus back to her current predicament and the need to find a way out of it.

Tamryn peered toward the western sky. It was already melting into a mixture of orange and pink as the sun was gradually swallowed up by the horizon. Which should she fear more, getting on that bike with Mr. Sexy Dimples or getting eaten by some swamp creature? She'd already determined that she was over those tingles, so the choice was simple.

"I'll take you up on your ride," Tamryn said. She immediately cringed. Was she hearing sexual innuendo even where there was none?

A faint smile lifted the corners of his lips. "Smart choice," he said.

That remained to be seen. If her too-often-ignored libido decided to come out and play, Tamryn was sure she would regret not trying her luck with the swamp creatures.

"I'll need to take my laptop," she told him.

"You don't have to worry about anyone stealing it. This road doesn't get much traffic."

She tossed a look over her shoulder. "You're on it."

His grin edged up just a bit more. "Touché."

It occurred to her that he obviously had no idea who she was. Tamryn wasn't sure how she felt about that. It was probably a good thing, seeing as the man had made an

Olympic sport out of avoiding her, but there was a teeny, tiny portion of her ego that was just a teeny, tiny bit ticked off. Seriously, they'd played phone tag and exchanged emails since last fall. Was a little recognition too much to ask for?

Although it was quite possible that he hadn't taken the time to scour the internet for information about her. She, on the other hand, had spent the better part of the past semester trying to learn all she could about Matthew Gauthier's family and the sleepy little town along the Louisiana bayou that one of his ancestors founded nearly two centuries ago. To say she had become a bit obsessed would occupy the top spot of the Understatement of the Century list.

Tamryn opened the car and grabbed hold of her purse and the messenger bag that doubled as her laptop case.

Before she even had the chance to close the door, Matthew had already plucked the bag from her fingers and pulled the strap over his head and across his chest. Then he walked over to the bike and climbed on.

His hands gripping the handlebars, he gestured her over with his head. "Hop on."

Tamryn peered down at her sage-green silk shell, gray pencil skirt and heels.

Well, this will be interesting.

She walked the remaining couple of feet to the huge motorcycle. With a deep breath, she hitched her skirt up about an inch and tried to climb onto the bike. She was barely able to part her legs. She drew her skirt a bit higher, but it was still way too snug.

Matt peered over his shoulder. "You need some help?"

"No," Tamryn quickly assured him. "I've got it."

Pushing back a tidal wave of self-consciousness, she hiked her skirt up to the very tops of her thighs and, capturing the hand he held out to her, climbed onto the massive machine. She latched on to the sides of the seat, steadying herself.

Was the tremble quaking throughout her stomach due to this being her first time on a motorcycle or because of her proximity to the bike's other occupant?

Matt unhooked the helmet from the handlebar and handed it to her. "It's too big for you, but it's better than nothing."

"Thanks," Tamryn said. She donned the helmet, cringing at how ridiculous she must look dressed in her best Professor Tamryn West, Ph.D., attire and wearing a motorcycle helmet. It was a good thing she wasn't vain.

"You'll need to hold on to me," he said.

Her eyes fell shut. She'd just *known* that

was coming.

Matt reached back with his left hand and captured her wrist, wrapping her arm around him. Tamryn brought her right arm in front and linked her hands together around his waist. She could feel the solid muscles of his abdomen underneath the soft cotton T-shirt, branding her palms.

Down, libido, she silently admonished. They were just abs, for goodness' sake. Very nice, very ripped abs, but still just abs.

He started the bike and the engine reverberated, rolling like thunder underneath them and adding to the quake in her belly.

"Don't go too fast," Tamryn called over his shoulder.

She could feel his low rumble of laughter against her hands, but he heeded her request, setting out on a leisurely ride. Despite their sedate pace, bits of rock and dust still kicked up from the tires, pelting her bare skin. By the time Matt turned off the dirt road and onto smooth asphalt, her legs were burning. She knew she'd have a few nicks and scratches.

They rode for several miles, driving past quaint clapboard houses. Some had large wraparound porches, and just about all of them had huge front yards.

A few minutes later, they turned onto a

21

driveway, which led up to the magnificent yellow Victorian home Tamryn had fallen in love with when she'd booked her stay online. It had white trim, a conical turret and a classic pitched roof.

Just as they pulled up to the front porch, the door opened and a woman who looked to be about Tamryn's age walked out.

"Hey, there, Matt," she called with a wave.

"How's it going, Phil? I found one of your guests stranded on the road that leads to Ponderosa Pond."

"Uh-oh. What happened?" the woman asked as she hurried down the steps.

At the moment, Tamryn's main concern was getting off the bike without flashing her goodies to the world. She hiked her skirt up and quickly slipped off, pushing her skirt down as soon as her feet touched the ground.

"A busted radiator on my rental car," she answered. She pulled off the helmet and handed it to Matt. "Thank you."

"You're welcome," he answered. The sudden lower pitch to his voice was not helping in her quest to keep the tingles at bay.

"Sorry about the car trouble," the other woman said. "Not a good way to start your vacation." She held her hand out. "I'm Phylicia, by the way. We talked on the phone the other day."

"Oh, yes. I'm Tamryn," she said, shaking the woman's outstretched hand.

"I figured. All of our other guests have already checked in. Let's get you inside. I just made a pitcher of lemonade. Matt, you want any?"

They both looked back at Matt, who was still on the motorcycle. Tamryn was momentarily stunned by the power he exuded, his firm thighs braced apart as he steadied himself on the bike.

Instead of getting off, he put on the helmet Tamryn had just handed him and secured the chin strap. "I'll go back and get her bags," he said.

"That's really not necessary," she told him. "I can drive back to get them once the rental company brings me a replacement car."

"Or I can send Jamal," Phylicia suggested. "He's at his office in New Orleans, but should be getting home soon."

"I already know where the car is," Matt said. He held his hand out to her. "Keys?"

"Are you sure?" Tamryn asked him.

"Very sure," he answered. "Let me have your keys."

His eyes were the only part of his face visible from behind the helmet and lower face shield, but she could tell by the way they crinkled at the corners that he was smiling.

She pulled the single key from the pocket of her slim skirt and dropped it into his palm.

"I won't be gone too long." His voice did that sexy, deepening thing again, and her body responded in kind.

This was not good. It wasn't even in the neighborhood of good.

She'd come to Gauthier in hopes of getting to know this man better . . . in a *professional* way. There was nothing professional about the fireworks that went off in her belly whenever his voice dropped low.

Matt revved the bike's engine and, with a brief nod and another of those inconceivably sexy grins, took off down the driveway. Tamryn continued to stare until he was nothing more than a small dot on the horizon.

"If you'd like, I can show you to your room, then you can come down to dinner," Phylicia said, knocking her out of her daze.

Tamryn turned to her, embarrassed by the fact that she didn't have a clue what the woman had just said. "I'm sorry, but what was that?"

Phylicia's lips held a trace of a grin. "He has that effect on people," she said. "Anyway, as I was saying, dinner is at seven. It's communal and held in the large dining room, but if you'd like, I can bring your food to your room. Room service isn't something we offer, but after the afternoon you've had, you're probably not up for dining with a bunch of people you don't know. You look as if you can use some rest."

"Is it that bad?" Tamryn asked, running a self-conscious hand through her hair.

Phylicia's lips twisted with chagrin. "Sorry, I'm still learning how to be a gracious hostess who doesn't speak her mind all the time."

"That's okay." Tamryn laughed. "I'd rather hear the truth."

She'd checked in through Belle Maison's online service before arriving, so Phylicia, who she learned was the fiancée of the bed-and-breakfast's owner, showed her to her room. It was elegantly furnished, with a four-poster canopy bed, a tufted settee with delicate legs and a cheval mirror in the corner. She'd chosen this room specifically for the balcony that overlooked the gazebo on the east lawn. She rarely got the chance to enjoy working outside, and Tamryn planned to spend most of her summer on the reclining patio chair she spotted out there.

As much as she wanted to explore where she would be residing for the next month and a half, the first thing Tamryn did once Phylicia left was go straight to the bathroom at the end of the hallway. She had been dying to wash off the bits of dirt that had glommed on to her legs during her motorcycle ride into town.

After cleaning up, she returned to her room and fished the number for the car-rental company from her purse. Tamryn was standing outside on her balcony, trying to maintain her patience as she waited for the customer-service representative to come back on the line, when she noticed a jet-black Mercedes-Benz turning into the driveway. It pulled closer to the house and out of her line of vision.

A few minutes later there was a knock on her door. She opened it to find Matt loaded down with her luggage.

"Where can I put these?" he asked.

Just as she was about to answer, the customer-service rep came back on the line. Tamryn pointed to the area in front of the bed and held her finger up, asking him to wait.

"I already told you that the road where the car is located didn't have any signs. It was just a dirt road," she told the woman

26

on the other end of the line.

Matt gestured for her to give him the phone. Her brows hitched, silently asking, *Are you sure?* He nodded and crooked his fingers. She handed him the phone and crossed her arms over her chest, eager to see if he would be able to make any progress.

"Hello," he spoke into the phone. His voice was incredibly smooth and vastly different from the clipped tone he'd used when rushing her off the phone the few times she'd been able to get past the office manager at his law firm.

"Do you have your own towing service, or do you contract out to the closest local company?" he asked the customer-service rep. "I figured as much. If you're going with Beauregard's Towing, it'll probably be Wayne who gets the call. Just tell him it's the road off of Highway 421 that leads to Ponderosa Pond. He'll know where to find the car." He nodded again. "I'm sure. Tell him to call this number if he has any problems." He rattled off a phone number and handed the phone back to Tamryn.

"Uh . . . yeah," Tamryn stammered. "Did you get all that?" The woman confirmed the directions and told her another rental car would be delivered by tomorrow morning.

"Thank you," Tamryn said before hanging up. She turned to Matt. "And thank *you*. I've spent the past twenty minutes trying to explain where I left the car. I don't know if you were going for your merit badge, but you've definitely earned it today."

He held three fingers above his brow in the Boy Scout salute. Then he smiled again. It was slow and easy, and just a little bit devastating.

For several moments they just stood there staring at each other. Normally, she would have felt awkward, but for some reason, she didn't. Maybe because it was hard to feel anything past the excited charge rushing through her bloodstream.

It was the dimples. The dimples were killing her.

"Thanks for bringing my bags," Tamryn said, gesturing to the luggage, but not breaking eye contact. "You really didn't have to do that. I've interrupted your day enough already."

"It was a welcome interruption." His eyes sparkled with a sexy mischief that did nothing to subdue the attraction she was trying to pretend wasn't there. He paused for a beat, then asked, "Would you like to go to dinner?"

Tamryn's head reared back slightly.

So he's not a fan of subtlety.

"There's dinner here," she said.

Another flash of that smile. Tamryn was stunned at how readily it came, especially when she considered how unfriendly he'd seemed the few times she'd spoken to him on the phone. She liked this Matthew Gauthier a thousand times more than the one who'd thwarted her attempts to communicate for the past six months.

"I'm sure there's nothing wrong with Phil's cooking," he said. He took a couple of steps toward her, reached forward and captured her wrist. He ran his thumb lazily back and forth over the pulse there, and for Tamryn, breathing suddenly became the most difficult thing in the world.

"However," Matt continued, "I can think of a few other places where we can have a nice, quiet meal together. Maybe enjoy a glass of wine while you tell me what brought you to our cozy little town. Why don't you let me take you to dinner?"

Her entire being screamed *yes,* but thankfully, she still possessed the good sense to shake her head in the negative.

"I'm sorry, but I can't," Tamryn said.

"Are you sure?"

She nodded. "It's been such a long day."

And the last time she'd called him, he'd

threatened to file harassment charges against her. She could only assume that the dinner invitations would not be forthcoming once he realized just whom he'd invited to dinner.

There was also the fact that all she really knew about him were the few tidbits she'd unearthed during her internet searches, and the fact that his ass looked spectacular in denim. And the dimples. Couldn't forget about the dimples.

She couldn't forget her purpose for being here, either. She'd come to Louisiana to work. She would love to sit down with Matthew Gauthier for a few hours and talk, but wine and candlelight dinners could not be a part of the equation.

"It just wouldn't be a good idea," Tamryn stated.

A touch of disappointment ghosted over his face, but then the smile returned. "You *have* had an eventful introduction to Gauthier," he said. "Tomorrow, then? Or at least sometime before you leave town. My good deed warrants at least a dinner, doesn't it?"

Her arms crossed over her chest, Tamryn cocked her head to the side. "You didn't tell me there would be a price when you offered me a ride."

His eyes, which she realized were a remarkable shade of hazel and green, sparkled with amusement. "You didn't ask."

She refused to let that smile affect her.

"What if I'm not willing to pay your asking price? Will you haul me onto that bike and drop me back in the middle of nowhere?"

"Won't be necessary," he said. "You'll eventually agree to dinner."

Her brow lifted. "You sound so confident."

He didn't answer, just continued to grin with that cocky self-assuredness as he backed out of the room.

Tamryn walked over to the door and continued to stare as he made his way down the hallway. He looked back at her, the overconfident grin still in place.

Oh, yeah. This would definitely be an interesting summer.

CHAPTER 2

Matthew Gauthier searched through the chaos cluttering his desk, lifting files and thumbing through mail that had lingered unopened for well over a week.

"Matt, are you still there?"

"I'm here," he called in the direction of his cell, which lay on his desk in speaker-phone mode. "Why didn't you leave the papers with Carmen? You know she's better at keeping track of things than I am."

"Because you told me to leave them on your desk," Benjamin Keller answered. "If you have a chance in hell of getting through this campaign successfully, you will have to get it together, Matt."

"Yes, yes, I know." Matt ran across a file he'd been looking for last week, and underneath it found the forms his campaign manager had left on his desk. "I found them."

"Thank God." Ben's sigh came through

the phone.

Matt had made public his plans to run for the state-senate seat in his district some time ago, but had held off filing the paperwork until today. He would drive out to Baton Rouge this afternoon so he could officially file with the state.

"Log in to instant messenger," Ben said. "I'm sending you a link to a YouTube commercial your future opponent's camp released today."

"Another one?"

Matt ran a hand down his face, cursing as he turned to his computer. He clicked on the link as soon as the message bubble popped up. The video began with a baby screaming at the top of his lungs and the words *Little Matthew Gauthier just keeps whining* in bold print across the bottom.

Matt's blood pressure escalated as the commercial continued. It was the same old crap his opponent, Patrick Carter, had been spouting since the moment Matt made it known that he would run for the state-senate seat that had become available following a bribery scandal the former senator had become embroiled in. Carter was a career politician who was used to running unopposed for whatever public office he deemed worthy of his greatness. The man had held nearly every political seat there was.

In this latest ad, Carter attacked Matt's age, claiming that at thirty-two, Matt was still too wet behind the ears to do any good for the people of District Twelve. But what really pissed him off was his opponent's insistence that because Matt had been born into Gauthier's wealthiest family, he couldn't possibly understand the struggles the rest of the residents faced. He would not allow Carter to pull that silver-spoon-in-the-mouth bullshit on him.

"I'm not even officially in the race yet," Matt said.

"He's doing this because he knows you're a threat," Ben replied. "You know what this means, right?"

"Forget it, Ben." Matt put his elbows on his desk and massaged his temples. "I already told you I'm not stooping to Carter's level."

"Dammit, Matt, when are you gonna listen to me? Politics is a dirty business. If you want to win this seat, you'll need to sling some mud. Stop trying to be the stand-up candidate. That candidate never wins."

"He will this time," Matt said. "Don't worry about Carter. The people here can see right through him."

"Really?" Ben drawled. "If that's the case, how has he been able to hold nearly every public seat in local government?"

Ben had a point.

Unable to come up with an adequate response to his campaign manager's very valid argument, Matt said, "Be here at three so we can leave for Baton Rouge." He ended the call with Ben and buzzed his office manager, Carmen Mitchell. "Carmen, can you get me the file for Mrs. Black's case? I think the insurance company is about to cave."

"Will do," Carmen said.

Matt pushed his chair away from the desk and stood, luxuriating in a total-body stretch. It was just after 10:00 a.m., yet it felt as if he'd already put in a full day. He knew he should have started turning down cases when he'd made the decision to run for office months ago, but his was the only law practice in town. In fact, for more than a century and a half, the Gauthier Law Firm had been the only means for legal representation in a twenty-mile radius. How could he turn anyone away?

He thumbed through the messages Carmen had handed him when he'd come in this morning and ran across at least one person he was pretty good at turning away. He crumpled the green slip of paper with yet another message from that nosy Professor West and tossed it in the trash.

The woman had been the biggest pain in his ass for the past six months. Ever since it had been discovered that this building had once been a part of the Underground Railroad, she'd been calling and emailing, digging her nose in his business. If not for all the stationery he'd have to replace, Matt would have changed the office's phone number.

He didn't have time to concern himself with Professor West right now; he had more than enough to worry about. The first item on his plate was to bring some semblance of order to his desk. Carmen had straightened it out yesterday. If she came in and saw the mess he'd made, there would be hell to pay.

Matt did his best to get the files back in order. He opened the bottom drawer and retrieved a can of the energy drink he kept stashed in there. As he chugged half the can in one large gulp, he replayed the YouTube video again, his jaw clenching as he watched the ridiculous commercial.

Carter might have more years on him, but he was the exact opposite of what the people in this area needed. He was one of Leroy Gauthier's old cronies. Matt's father and Patrick Carter had had a falling-out years ago, but the two men were cut from the same cloth. Their way of thinking tended to provide more benefits for themselves than their constituents. It was time for a change in the way politics was played around here.

Carmen gave two short raps on the door before she entered the office, carrying a file.

"Thanks," he said as he captured the beige folder she held out to him. His high-school English teacher, Mrs. Black, was suing the school system's health-insurance company for lack of coverage. Matt wanted to read through the file again before his telephone call with the school board's attorney.

He looked up at Carmen, who'd remained standing in front of his desk.

"Yeah?" Matt asked.

"You have a visitor," she said. The smile tipping up the corner of her mouth sent a tremor of unease down his spine.

"Who is it?" he asked, hoping to God it wasn't his father. Although his father would never wait in the lobby like a guest. He'd officially passed the Gauthier mansion on to Matt, but the old man still took owner-ship of this office. It didn't matter that he hadn't practiced law here since becoming an appellate-court judge in New Orleans several years ago.

"It's Professor Tamryn West," Carmen answered.

"What?" Matt shot out of his chair. "You're kidding me."

"I am not," Carmen said. "Should I send her in?"

"No." He came around the desk. "What the hell is she doing here? Doesn't she teach somewhere up on the East Coast?"

"Boston," Carmen answered. "The woman came all this way, Matt. You *have* to see her."

"No, I don't."

Carmen gave him a look. He hated that damn look. It was the same look his mother used to give him when she thought he was being stubborn.

"Shit," Matt cursed. "Send her in. But if she's not gone in five minutes, you'd better make up some excuse and come rescue me, Carmen. I mean it."

She laughed. "What are you so afraid of when it comes to this professor?"

"Nothing. I just don't like people snooping around in my business."

"Fine. But she traveled well over a thousand miles. The least you can do is give her ten minutes of your time."

"Seven," Matt countered. "If she's not gone in seven minutes, I want you to bang on the door and yell *fire.*"

Carmen shook her head, still laughing.

Matt went around his desk and sat, then immediately sprang from the seat. He didn't want to feel as if he was at a disadvantage when he faced an adversary. He went around to the front of the polished oak desk that had occupied this office for the past sixty years and perched against it, crossing his feet at the ankles.

Carmen knocked on the door and opened it. "Professor Tamryn West is here to see you," she announced.

Matt's stomach bottomed out as he stared at the woman who'd just walked into his office. "You have *got* to be kidding me."

"*You're* Dr. West?"

Tamryn just barely held in the laugh that was precariously close to spilling from her lips. The look of shock on Matthew Gauthier's face was priceless.

The rest of him looked . . . amazing.

Yesterday's jeans and black T-shirt had been the stuff of carefully choreographed fantasies, but this morning's charcoal-gray suit, Tiffany-blue shirt and striped tie were fantasy-worthy in their own right.

"Good morning to you, too, Mr. Gauthier," Tamryn said. She strode over to the desk that occupied the center of the vast office, stopping a couple of feet in front of him.

"Good morning," he said with a note of apology, as if he'd been reprimanded for forgetting his manners. "*You're* Tamryn West?" he asked again.

She nodded and extended her hand out to him. "Dr. Tamryn West, professor of African-American and women's studies at Brimley College."

He accepted her handshake, disappointment and disbelief clouding his face.

The office manager, who had introduced herself as Carmen, cleared her throat. "It looks as if my employer has misplaced his manners," she said. "Can I offer you a seat, Dr. West?"

"Thank you," Tamryn said.

"Yes, I'm . . . I'm sorry," Matt said. He shook his head as if to clear it and gestured to one of the high-backed leather chairs. "Carmen, is there coffee?" He looked to her. "Would you like coffee?"

"I'm fine." She waved off the offer.

"Well, I'll leave you two," Carmen said as she backed out of the office.

Matt's brow dipped as he studied Tamryn

for several moments before rounding the desk and settling into the chair behind it. The brown leather gleamed, but it was obvious from the many cracks and faded spots that it was well used. He picked up a pen, tapped it twice on a thick file folder and then tossed it onto the desk.

"I never put two and two together," he said with a bemused shake of his head. "Even after you told me your name yesterday, I still didn't make the connection."

"I must admit that I didn't recognize you right away, either," Tamryn said. "In the few pictures I found of you online, you were always in a suit and tie, never on a Harley."

"Ducati."

"Excuse me?"

"My bike is a Ducati, not a Harley." He waved it off. "Never mind."

"Well, whatever the brand of motorcycle, I never pictured you on one. Coupled with the fact that I was beyond exhausted and frustrated, it isn't all that surprising that I didn't recognize you right off the bat."

And in those few online pictures she *had* found, never once had he been smiling. If he had been, those dimples would have been a dead giveaway.

"But you did recognize me after a while?" Matt asked.

She nodded.

"Well, if you recognized me, why didn't you say anything yesterday?"

Tamryn couldn't contain her wry smile. She crossed her legs and folded her hands over her knee.

"You've spent the past six months avoiding me. I was afraid you would leave me out on the side of the road if you knew I was the professor you've been thwarting at every turn."

An offended frown tugged down the corners of his mouth. "I never would have left you out there."

Tamryn held her hands up. "Forgive me. That was a poor attempt at humor. I know you wouldn't have left me stranded. Thank you again for coming to my rescue yesterday." She tipped her head to the side. "You must admit it's rather funny that the only person I have any knowledge of in Gauthier just so happened to be the one who found me. Either this town really is that small, or it's an amazing coincidence."

A hint of amusement flashed in his light brown eyes. "Maybe a little of both," he said. "Believe it or not, I almost didn't go for a ride yesterday. I decided at the last minute that I needed to clear my head and just hopped on the bike almost without thinking." His penetrating gaze eased its way along her body. "It's as if I was meant to find you."

His voice resonated with meaning, evoking a shimmer of interest that cascaded along her exposed skin. Tamryn surreptitiously sucked in a breath as she straightened in her chair and damned her tingling spine to hell.

The laugh that escaped her throat was much huskier than she'd intended. "Interesting how that turned out, isn't it?"

He nodded slowly, reclining in his chair. "Very."

His stare was probing and filled with enough heat to sear her skin. Usually, being on the receiving end of such intense scrutiny would creep her out. This time it did the exact opposite.

Tamryn cleared her throat and twisted yet again in her seat.

"So, what brings you here?" Matt asked, folding his hands over those abs that her fingers already had intimate knowledge of. "I doubt you came all this way simply because I've been avoiding your calls."

"No," she said, shaking her head. "You're important to my research, but not that important."

His brows lifted. "So you're here doing

research?"

"For the entire summer," she answered.

He groaned and ran a hand down his face.

"How quickly that charm disappears when you put on a suit and tie. Maybe you should come to the office in a T-shirt and jeans."

"Forgive me," he said, straightening once again and running a smoothing hand down his tie. "If my old nanny were still alive, she would have plucked me on the ear for being so rude."

"Happy to know I bring out the worst in you," Tamryn teased.

"You just took me by surprise showing up here at my office," he said. "Although, now that I think about it, I shouldn't be surprised at all to see you in Gauthier. To say that you are persistent, Dr. West, is an understatement."

"I can deal with being called persistent. I've been called worse."

"I'm not sure I believe that. Now that I've met you, I can think of a dozen more appropriate adjectives that would apply."

The lazy grin that traveled across his lips caused all manner of naughty things to stir within her belly.

This was so not what she had predicted when she'd imagined her first face-to-face meeting with Matthew Gauthier. Based on his evasiveness these past few months, she'd prepared herself for adversarial at best, but had been expecting downright caustic.

What she had *not* expected were those killer dimples or that smooth-as-butter voice. She surely had not anticipated having to practice keeping her heart rate at a reasonable level while in close proximity to him.

"What is it that led you to Gauthier?"

"I'm researching the Underground Railroad," Tamryn answered.

"I know that from your many, many, *many* phone calls and emails," he said, softening the veiled reprimand with another infectious grin. "But why make the trip all the way down here? There's a professor at Tulane University who is working on this already. He's put much of what he's found online. You could have just connected with him and saved yourself a lot of time and money."

"Actually, I've been in contact with Professor Lawrence since the discovery was made. I find the work he's doing with his students fascinating, but this is something I need to see with my own eyes. My research is in a different vein from that of Professor Lawrence's. I have a lot of my own questions."

"I've hardly ventured to that side of the building since they started digging around over there," he said. "I'm sorry to break this to you, but I won't be much help."

"How do you know how much help you'll be? I haven't asked any questions yet."

He choked out a shocked laugh. "You haven't asked any questions? What about those many, *many* emails?"

She waved him off. "That was just a little harmless digging."

His eyes brightened with amusement. "Harmless, huh? Does that mean what you have next up your sleeve is going to cause me some real pain?"

There was a single knock at the door before it opened. The office manager poked her head in. "Excuse me," she said.

Tamryn looked over at Matt just in time to see him subtly shake his head.

A knowing grin flashed across her face as she turned to the office manager. "Let me guess, he told you to come in and rescue him in ten minutes?"

"Actually, it was five," the woman answered.

Matt shot her a bland look. "Thanks a lot, Carmen."

"And I'm not rescuing you," she said. "I wanted to make sure you have everything you need for the conference call on Mrs. Black's case."

"I do. Thanks." He rose from behind his desk, buttoning his jacket. It fit his frame to perfection, molding to those muscular shoulders that had been displayed underneath his T-shirt yesterday. He rounded the desk and gestured with his head for Tamryn to follow. "I'm going to take Professor West on a short tour of the building so she can see the room that was unearthed last summer. If the attorney representing the school board's health insurance calls early, please come get me. It took weeks just to set up this call."

He held the door open. "After you," he said to Tamryn.

She slipped past him, then waited for him to lead her down a somewhat narrow, paneled hallway. It was obvious that the building was old, but it was also well preserved.

"The room is still the equivalent of an archaeological dig site," Matt called over his shoulder. "It's been roped off since it was confirmed that it was an actual stop on the Underground Railroad. I doubt I'll ever get my entire building back."

"It's not yours anymore," Tamryn said.

He stopped and turned. "Whose is it?"

"This type of history belongs to everyone. You can't claim ownership anymore."

"But I can pay the property tax on it?"

"Consider it your small part in preserving the past," she said.

He shook his head, his soft chuckle reverberating in the air around her. "You sure you chose the right field of study, Professor West? Maybe you should have been an attorney."

"Never once considered law," she answered. "History is my . . . passion." Tamryn's voice trailed off as she stepped into the darkened room, her eyes trained on the far wall, where another door was open, but cordoned off by several strips of yellow caution tape.

She walked slowly up to the entrance, her lungs constricting as she came upon the tiny room. Tamryn brought trembling fingers to her lips, willing herself to keep it together. She'd vowed she was not going to cry.

But how could she not be overrun with emotion? Her great-great-great-grandmother had likely been in this very room — not as a slave fleeing to the freedom that awaited in the North, but as a conductor, assisting others on the Underground Railroad. Everything she'd uncovered over the years that she'd spent researching Adeline West indicated that she had ushered hundreds of slaves out of this area.

"Are you okay?"

Tamryn jumped at Matthew's softly struck question. She hastily wiped at the moisture dampening her cheeks as she turned and smiled up at him.

"I'm fine," she said. "I guess I wasn't prepared for how this would affect me." She wrapped her arms around her waist and hunched her shoulders. "I've seen dozens of sites like this, and I'm always overwhelmed."

The sound of footsteps tapping on the hardwood could be heard for a few seconds before Carmen appeared. "Matt, the school board's attorney is on the line."

He held his hand up. "I'll be there in a minute, Carmen."

"No, go ahead," Tamryn said. "I appreciate the quick tour. I've spoken to Dr. Lawrence, and he's invited me to join him when he returns." She swiped at her cheeks again. "However, I would like to set up an interview with you."

"Me?" His eyes widened. "Why me?"

"Well, you're a Gauthier, for one thing. Your family founded this town."

"The Gauthiers who founded this town died a long time ago, and unfortunately, I'm not what you would call a history buff. I won't be able to tell you anything that you can't find out on your own."

"That's not necessarily true," Tamryn

said. "It all depends on the questions I ask. I'll bet you know more than you think you do."

He buried his hands in his pockets and sucked in an uneasy breath.

"Look, there was a pamphlet created for Gauthier's anniversary celebration this past summer. Ask Carmen to put you in touch with Mya Dubois-Anderson. She'll be able to tell you everything you need to know."

"But —"

Carmen came to the door again. "Matt, do you want me to have the attorney call back in a half hour?"

"No," he said. "I'm coming." He turned back to Tamryn. "Sorry, but this is the end of the tour. Carmen will see you out."

And with that he took off, leaving Tamryn with even more questions than she'd had when she first walked through the door.

CHAPTER 3

Matt ended the call with the school board's attorney with a promise to see the man in court if he could not come up with a better settlement for Mrs. Black's case. He could tell by the stunned silence on the other end of the line that the man had not expected a small-town lawyer to take such a hard line. Matt had encountered such attitudes more times than he could count over the years.

He sat back in his chair and closed his eyes. As he listened to the faint gurgle of Heritage Park's landmark wooden waterwheel churning a few yards outside his open window, one question continued to swirl around in his head.

Why?

Why had the woman he'd gone to bed dreaming about last night showed up in his office this morning looking like everything he could ever want . . . and everything he had been trying to avoid? This had to go

51

down as the most ironic twist of fate in the history of all mankind.

He'd spent an unhealthy portion of last night coming up with various scenarios that would have him coincidentally showing up at Belle Maison. After a while, he'd decided that he didn't have the time or patience for devising fake, coincidental meetings. The chemistry that had sparked between him and Tamryn yesterday made scheming un-necessary. He'd already made the decision to drive over to the B and B after work and extend another dinner invitation to its new-est guest.

As of this morning, everything had changed.

Discovering that the beauty he'd rescued yesterday was the same woman who posed a significant threat to everything he held dear rewrote all the plans his overactive imagination had concocted. The moment he learned she was the same Tamryn West who had been digging into his family's his-tory, Matt knew any plans to pursue her were null and void.

Well, his brain knew it. He needed other parts of his body to get the memo.

Running a frustrated hand down his face, he checked the time on his computer just as his stomach let out a loud growl. Maybe if he'd fed it more than an energy drink this morning it wouldn't be so angry with him.

Matt slipped his cell phone into his pocket and strode out of his office.

He rapped his knuckles on the door to the file room, where Carmen stood before an open cabinet drawer. "I'm heading to the bank and then over to Emile's for a quick bite. You want anything?"

"Yes," Carmen said, shutting the drawer with her hip and walking toward him. "I want to know what's up with you and Professor West."

Matt's forehead creased in a frown as he followed her out of the file room. "There's nothing up with me and Professor West."

Carmen tossed the manila folder on the desk, then perched on the edge of it. "For a lawyer, you are a horrible liar, Matthew Gauthier."

"I'm not lying. I have no idea what you're talking about."

"Don't give me that." She pointed toward his office. "There was more chemistry in there than in the science lab at Gauthier High School. What's going on with you two? Did you know she would be here?"

"Hell no. Didn't you see how shocked I was to see her standing in my office?"

She crossed her arms over her chest and

continued to stare at him. Carmen Mitchell had only been two years ahead of him in high school, but she'd become his father's secretary right after she graduated, which meant she had more than a dozen years' seniority over Matt at the Gauthier Law Firm. It was something she never let him forget, despite the fact that he was technically her boss.

Matt blew out a tired breath. "Okay, so I met her last night," he admitted. "But I didn't know who she was at the time. I was out for a ride on my bike and found her stranded with a car that had a busted radiator. She's staying at Belle Maison. I brought her there, then went back for her bags."

"And you didn't realize she was the same Tamryn West who's been calling here every week for the past six months?"

"How was I supposed to know she was the same woman? I had no idea what she looked like."

"Oh, come on, Matt. I knew who she was the second she walked through the door. Haven't you heard of Google?"

"I never thought to look her up online." And he was sorry he hadn't. He would have been better prepared to handle the shock he'd had when she waltzed through his door this morning. He sure as hell hadn't visualized *that* when he'd pictured the professor who had been making a pest of herself all these months.

He'd taken torts with a Professor West back in law school, and whenever Tamryn West's email popped up in his inbox, that was who he pictured. The wrinkle-faced, bald-headed white guy was the exact opposite of the woman who'd left his office a couple of hours ago.

"She's even more gorgeous in person," Carmen mused. "Maybe you should ask her to dinner."

"Be real, Carmen."

"What? You've been through all the single women in this town already."

"First of all, I have not been through all of the single women in Gauthier. And second . . ." Matt released a sigh. "I already asked her to dinner last night. She turned me down."

Carmen barked out a laugh. He didn't join in.

"It's a good thing we didn't go out last night," he reasoned. "It would have made things even more awkward this morning."

"She's always very pleasant when she calls. I still don't get why you're so stubborn when it comes to talking to her."

"I don't like people snooping in my business." Carmen silently mimicked his words. Matt rolled his eyes. "Do you want anything from Emile's?" he asked again.

"Only if they have bread pudding for dessert. Oh, wait a sec." She reached for a parcel of envelopes on her desk and thumbed through them, handing one to him. "Give this to Theresa at the bank. She'll know what to do with it."

Matt took the envelope and left Carmen with a promise to return in an hour. He walked along Main Street, Gauthier's central attraction. Despite the slight breeze that ruffled the purplish-pink petals of the saucer magnolia trees lining the street, the humidity had him wishing he'd left his suit jacket back at his office.

Like his family's law practice, many of the other businesses along Main Street had served this small community for well over a century. Matt strolled past Cannon's Dry Cleaner's and the Gauthier Pharmacy and Feed Store on his way to Gauthier Bank and Trust. The bank had long been taken over by a larger regional chain, but after an uproar over plans to change the logo and remove the ornamental clock that had hung over the bank's entrance for more than 150 years, the corporate offices had agreed to make an exception. The checks and debit cards had the chain's name and logo, but the sign and clock out front remained the same.

He entered the bank and spotted Theresa Rushing behind the counter. He and Theresa had graduated together from Gauthier High School.

"Hey there, Matt. How's the campaign going?" Theresa greeted.

"It hasn't officially kicked off yet, but my opponent is already slinging some heavy mud."

"That's a good sign. It means he's taking you seriously, which he very well should. Patrick Carter has been in office too long already. He'll probably run for dogcatcher after you whip his butt in this election."

"That's probably the only seat he hasn't held," Matt agreed with a laugh. He handed over the envelope. "Carmen said you'd know what to do with this. And I want to deposit this into the Katherine Gauthier fund," he added, slipping Theresa the money he'd drawn from his private equity account. He used his dividend checks to fund the account he'd set up in his mother's name to sponsor various charitable projects around Gauthier.

"No problem," she said. She cast a sly smile in his direction. "By the way, a *very*

57

nice-looking woman came in asking about you not too long ago. If I wasn't happily married, I would be jealous that some newcomer is scoping out Gauthier's most eligible bachelor."

Matt's stomach dropped. "Was she wearing a red top and black skirt?"

"Yeah," Theresa confirmed.

Dammit.

"What did she want to know?"

"Just stuff." She shrugged. "Whether or not you've lived in Gauthier your entire life. How long you've been practicing law in your grandfather's old building. Stuff like that. So." Theresa raised her brows. "Is she someone special?"

"Yeah, a special pain in my ass," Matt muttered. "Any idea where she went?"

"I think she said she was heading to Claudette's."

"Aw, shit." Anywhere but the beauty parlor. "I'll come back later for the deposit receipt. Or better yet, have someone bring it over to Carmen at the office."

"No problem," she called.

Matt quickly made it out of the bank and across the street to Claudette's Beauty Parlor. He opened the screen door and was nearly bowled over by all the estrogen. He usually avoided this place at all costs, mainly

58

because he'd dated two of the beauticians who worked here.

Dread crept up his spine as he spotted Tamryn sitting in one of the twirling salon chairs, her lean legs crossed. His gut clenched at the sight. It had done the same thing this morning when she'd assumed a similar position across from his desk.

"Well, look who's here," Claudette Robinson called, waving a comb at him.

"Hi, ladies," Matt greeted.

Joelle Richardson gave him a wave from where she stood at one of the shampooing basins along the back wall, washing someone's hair. Mariska Thomas grunted at him and rolled her eyes.

Things had ended amicably with Joelle. With Mariska, not so much.

"We were just telling Tamryn here about you running for state senate," Claudette said.

"They sure were." An amused glint lit up her eyes. "They also told me about your work with the Boys and Girls Club, and the scholarship you award at the high school, and the work you do with the elderly. You really *are* a Boy Scout, aren't you, Matthew?"

"Everybody loves Matt around here," Claudette chimed in.

There was another grunt from the station where Mariska was slathering cream in a customer's hair and folding pieces of foil over it.

"Don't mind her," Claudette said. In a loud whisper she pointed a finger between Matt and Mariska. "They used to date. Didn't end well."

"Oh." Tamryn's eyes widened in what looked like genuine curiosity. That expression alone told Matt that he needed to get her the hell away from these wagging tongues as quickly as possible.

"Professor West, you mind if I talk to you outside?" Matt asked.

"Professor?" Claudette's brows met her dyed hairline. "You didn't tell us you were a professor."

"I am." Tamryn unfolded those stunning legs and stood. "I teach African-American history and women's studies at a small liberal-arts college in Boston."

"Well, well, well. How very fancy," Claudette said. "I hope you enjoy your time in Gauthier. Stop by and see us again."

"I'm sure I will," Tamryn said as she slipped out the door Matt held open.

"What was that?" Matt asked as soon as they were outside.

"What was what?"

"Why are you going all over town asking about me?"

She put up a finger. "Okay, first of all, I am not going all over town asking about you. I've only been to the bank, the pharmacy and here."

"That's about all there is to Gauthier."

"And second —" her voice held a hint of irritation "— may I point out that I wouldn't have to go around asking about you if you'd just agree to an interview? I promise it'll be painless."

A nerve jumped in Matt's jaw. He was stuck between the proverbial rock and a hard place. He sure as hell didn't want to answer any of her prying questions, but if she insisted on digging into his background, he wanted to stay on top of just what she uncovered. There were things about both him and his family that were better left buried, and Matt intended on keeping it that way.

If he agreed to let her interview him, he could give her just enough to satisfy her curiosity. Maybe then she would move on to something else.

"Fine," Matt finally answered. "Why don't I take you to lunch? I'll answer anything you want to know."

She gave him a cheeky smile. "See, that

wasn't so hard, was it?"

Yeah, that was because the questions hadn't started yet.

"I knew I should have started dieting the day I decided to spend my summer in Louisiana," Tamryn said, using the crusty French bread to soak up some of the spicy shrimp étouffée. Her eyelids slid closed as she slipped the morsel between her lips, releasing a throaty moan.

Matt's stomach clenched at the sound. So did the fingers he'd wrapped around his glass of iced tea, to the point where he figured he was in danger of shattering the glass. She'd been making those little noises throughout their meal. Sounds that, if he closed his eyes, he could imagine coming from something much more enjoyable than a simple lunch at Emile's.

She expelled another satisfied sigh, then pushed the plate away. "No more. I can't spare the extra calories."

His eyes narrowed with his skeptical frown. "You're joking, right?"

"Oh, how I wish." She laughed, then hunched her shoulders in a hapless shrug. "What can I say? I love to eat. I'm counting this as my splurge meal for the week."

Matt shook his head. The woman clearly

worried about the wrong things.

From the moment he'd pulled his bike up to her smoking car yesterday, he hadn't been able to get her shapely body out of his head. The sleeveless top and formfitting skirt she wore today weren't helping.

Just picturing the way the slim black skirt conformed to her delicately curved hips and nicely rounded butt had his skin warming. She had the kind of legs you usually saw in lady-shaving-cream commercials, her calves toned and smooth. She stood about a half foot shorter than his own six feet three inches — just the right height. Their bodies would line up perfectly.

Whoa. That was an image he definitely didn't need in his head right now. He was having a hard enough time getting his body under control, especially after sitting here for the past twenty minutes watching as Tamryn wrapped her plump lips around her fork and moaned in pleasure with each bite.

Matt couldn't hold back his chagrin at the irony of it all. The woman he'd spent the past six months dodging every chance he could get was sitting across from him right now, eliciting the kind of wet dream–worthy fantasies he hadn't experienced since high school.

Eyeing the plate, Tamryn said, "One more

bite," before picking up the fork and scooping up more étouffée. She shoved the plate away again and tossed her linen napkin over the remnants of her lunch. "Okay, I'm really done now."

Matt lifted an amused brow. "You sure about that?"

"Yes. No more." She picked up her pen and notepad. "So, you've worked in your family's law practice since you finished law school?"

Matt squelched his disappointed sigh. He'd forgotten for a moment that, for her, this was a working lunch. If he used even an ounce of his common sense, he would accept that it should be the same for him. He'd already decided that any romantic interest in her was now off the table.

Although the longer he sat across from her, the harder it was to remember just why he could no longer pursue her.

"So?" she asked.

Matt straightened and blinked several times. "What?"

She sighed. "These questions are not that difficult, Mr. Gauthier."

"It's Matthew," he said. "Or Matt. And forgive me for being difficult."

"I didn't say that *you* were being difficult. I said that these questions were not. But now that you mention it, you *are* being rather difficult."

He grinned. "That's what happens when you strong-arm someone into an interview they didn't want to participate in."

She choked out a shocked laugh. "Strong-arm? Look at you and look at me. There is no way I could strong-arm you into doing anything you didn't want to do."

He folded his arms on the table and leaned toward her. "You don't need physical strength when you have that smile."

Matt didn't think it was possible for a person's cheeks to turn such a deep shade of crimson so quickly. He had to suppress the instant, overwhelming urge to taste the demure smile that formed on her lips.

"Thank you," she said, her cheeks still impossibly red, her face still impossibly gorgeous. She pointed to her notebook. "Can we get back to my list of questions?"

Suppressing his annoyance over her insistence on working, he made a circling motion with his hand. "Please proceed, Professor West."

"It's Tamryn," she said. "And I asked if you've worked in your family's law practice your entire career."

"For the most part," Matt answered, sitting back in his chair. "I clerked for the

Fifth Circuit Court of Appeals in New Orleans for a few years while still in law school."

"Your father is on that court, isn't he?"

"Yes. I guess you *have* done your research."

She waved him off with a flick of her wrist. "I was able to find out everything I needed to know about your father with a two-minute internet search. Leroy Gauthier has made some interesting rulings during his first few years as an appellate judge."

"If by 'interesting' you mean *controversial,* then yes," Matt answered.

"I was trying to be tactful."

Matt laughed. "*Tactful* and *Leroy Gauthier.* I doubt those words have ever been used together in a sentence before."

The corners of her mouth dipped with a curious frown, and Matt could practically see the wheels turning in her head with questions he wasn't up for answering.

"Anything else?" he asked. "You want to know about my mom? She died of cancer ten years ago."

"I read that, too," she said. "Her obituary was in the online archives of the local paper. I'm sorry about her passing."

Matt did his best to pull off an unaffected shrug. "She was more than ready to go.

She'd suffered for years."

The suffering his mother faced during her short bout with ovarian cancer was probably nothing compared to the misery she'd endured at the hands of her neglectful, adulterous husband. But that was something he certainly wasn't about to share with Tamryn West.

"I'm not really sure why you requested this meeting. It seems as if Google has told you everything you need to know."

"I want to know the things that Google *can't* tell me," Tamryn said.

Matt fingered a petal on one of the daisies in the slim vase in the center of the table. "And what is that, exactly?"

"Well, for instance, Google can't tell me what it was like being a member of the founding family of Gauthier. The town is named after you, for goodness' sake. Don't pretend it's not a big deal."

"The town is named after my great-great-uncle Micah Gauthier, not me. And I already told you that I'm not all that knowledgeable about my family's history." Matt shrugged. "I just don't have much interest in it."

Tamryn flattened her open palm to her chest. "Do you know how much that breaks my heart?"

"Sorry to be such a disappointment." Matt knew his grin contradicted his words.

"Once I'm done with my research I will probably know more about your family than you do," she said.

Her prediction caused an arrow of alarm to shoot down Matt's spine, because that was exactly what he most feared. There were things about his family that he didn't want *anyone* to know. He'd come from a long line of bootleggers, gamblers and worse. The town's founding family wouldn't be so revered if Gauthier's residents knew of his predecessors' past misdeeds.

If they knew of *his* misdeeds.

Matt leaned forward again and in a lowered voice said, "You know, there are better ways for you to spend your summer than researching my family."

The sexy smile that drew across her face had him thinking for a moment that he'd distracted her from her quest, until she said in an equally hushed voice, "I beg to differ. Your family is fascinating. You just don't understand because you haven't taken the time to delve into their history."

Matt sat back and released a defeated sigh. She might look like sex in high heels, but her prying was still a giant pain in his ass.

He held his palms up in a you-win gesture. "I don't know much about the Gauthier family's history, but I know the basics," he said. "Uncle Micah, who was part white, by the way, apparently won a bunch of land in a card game. I guess he was pretty self-important, because he decided there should be a town named after him. Thus, the town of Gauthier was born."

"From what I've read, Micah Gauthier was very generous. Calling him self-important doesn't seem fair."

Matt shrugged. "Never met him, so I can't be sure."

"You are absolutely no help at all."

"I told you I wouldn't be." He chuckled as he squeezed lemon juice into the iced tea the waiter had just refilled. He set the long teaspoon on the linen tablecloth and returned his attention to Tamryn. "Look, the history of this town is pretty much like the other towns in this area. I'll bet if folks look hard enough, they'll find other rooms like the one that was found in the law practice."

"Oh, I have no doubt," Tamryn said. "There are likely hundreds of secret hideaways that were used as part of the Underground Railroad that haven't been discovered throughout the South. It's always exciting when one is, which is why being here in Gauthier —"

The waiter returned to their table. "I'm sorry to interrupt again, but will you be enjoying dessert this afternoon? We have white-chocolate bread pudding and buttermilk pie."

"That sounds so good," Tamryn said. "But I can't."

"Oh, come on," Matt urged. "Dessert isn't just for special occasions around here. It's a part of every meal."

"Even breakfast?" she asked with a teasing smile.

"Damn right. Just wait until you have some beignets and café au lait."

She groaned. "If I'm not careful I will have to buy an entirely new, bigger wardrobe before the start of fall semester."

"You have nothing to worry about," Matt said. He looked up at the waiter. "Paul, can you box up a serving of bread pudding for me to take back to Carmen?"

"No problem, Matt. Oh, and I'm going to email you some artwork for the 5K T-shirts later tonight."

"Good. I need to get that to Mike's Printing over in Maplesville. He said the sooner we have the artwork, the sooner he can start making the T-shirts and yard signs."

When Paul left the table, Matt turned his

attention back to Tamryn. "Sorry about that."

"A 5K?" she asked.

Matt nodded, taking another sip of tea. "I — well, the Gauthier Law Firm — sponsors a yearly 5K to benefit the Gauthier Boys and Girls Summer Camp. It's turned into a pretty big event, much bigger than we ever expected it to become."

"Who's 'we'?"

"Carmen and I. She's the one who puts it together."

"But you foot the bill?"

He shrugged. "It's not much."

Tamryn folded her arms on the table and, with her head cocked to the side, studied him. He wasn't a fan of scrutiny, even when it involved a beautiful woman.

"What?" Matt asked.

"It wasn't just the talk of obviously smitten women at the beauty parlor. You really *are* a saint."

"Smitten? Do people really use that word?"

"There is no other way to describe them. All I had to do was bring up your name and off they went, talking about the food drive you sponsor for the elderly at Thanksgiving, and the Easter egg hunt for the children at the elementary school. And did I hear

71

something about a new tutor and mentorship program you've proposed for Gauthier High?"

He nodded.

"I can only assume that underneath that suit you're hiding a giant *S* on your chest."

Matt couldn't help the eye roll this time.

If she only knew. If *any* of them knew. He was far from a saint, or Superman, or any other hero this town deserved. He had his mother to thank for instilling in him a strong sense of compassion for his fellow man at an early age, but benevolence had very little to do with any of the things he did. Much of what he did for the people of Gauthier had to do with assuaging his own guilt.

"It's not as if I do any of it alone," he said. "It's a community effort. This is a small town. We take care of our own."

"I find that utterly charming," she said. "Everything about this town is charming. I'll have to sign up for the 5K you're sponsoring."

"You're a runner?" That explained the killer legs.

"I wouldn't consider myself a runner," she said with a laugh. "A moderately competent jogger is probably a better label. It's a great way to clear the mind. It also allows me to indulge in food I shouldn't eat."

"We'll have to go running sometime," Matt said.

"You run?"

"I do now."

That instant crimson stained her cheeks again, and the effect it had on him was downright frightening.

She was the last woman he wanted to affect him in any way whatsoever. She posed a direct threat to his future plans. If she succeeded in her mission of uncovering his family's past, he could kiss that state-senate seat goodbye.

Yet affect him she did. He was stunned and just a bit disturbed at the potency of his feelings. He'd been completely enraptured from the moment he'd spotted her walking along that dirt road.

Matt had already decided to keep an eye on her during her stay in Gauthier, but as he peered at her across the table, he acknowledged that keeping an eye on her wouldn't be the hardship he'd initially anticipated. In fact, he had the appealing suspicion that he would enjoy every minute of it.

As her pen traveled swiftly across the small memo pad she'd found in the bottom of her purse, Tamryn cursed herself for forgetting to bring her iPad. Of course, when she'd left the B and B this morning, she had not anticipated finally getting the chance to interview Matthew Gauthier one-on-one. During the course of an hour-long lunch, she'd managed to get more information out of him than from dozens of emails and phone calls over the past six months.

"What kind of special privileges come with being a member of the town's founding family?" she asked him.

"What makes you think I have special privileges just because I'm a Gauthier?"

"Well, I don't know. Maybe it's the opposite. Maybe being a Gauthier comes with lofty obligations. So, which is it? Do people expect more of you because of your family lineage? Is that why you're so involved with the community, because you have no other choice?"

He trained those hazel-green eyes on her and an easy smile drew up the corners of his mouth.

"Don't you think we've talked enough about me for today? Why don't you answer a few questions?"

"Because I'm the interviewer, not the interviewee."

"I'm turning the tables on you."

Tamryn set her pen on top of the memo pad and settled back in her chair, crossing her arms over her chest. "And just what could you possibly want to know about me?"

"Oh, there is so much I'd like to know about you, Professor West."

Seductive tremors traveled up and down her spine at the alluring lilt to his voice. That penetrating stare that seemed to look right through her only added to the trembles.

"However," he said, "you can start by telling me how you became interested in this subject."

The waiter came to their table and offered them coffee. Tamryn was grateful for the interruption. She needed the few moments to clear her head.

She also decided that, after occupying their table for so long, it was only fair to Emile's Restaurant that she order dessert to go. It was the easiest decision she'd made in at least a decade.

"So?" Matt asked as he added a teaspoon of sugar to his coffee. "What sparked your interest in this subject? Is it for one of the classes you're teaching or just because you're a history buff?"

She nodded as she sipped her coffee. "I'll

definitely incorporate my findings into my classes," she said. "However, my interest in Gauthier is related to another project, something much more personal."

One brow hitched in inquiry. "Too personal to share?"

"No." She shook her head. "Not anymore. A number of people know about the book I'm writing."

His eyes widened. "You're an author, too?"

"Nonfiction," she clarified. "Much of the research I'm conducting in Gauthier will go into a book I'm writing about my great-great-great-grandmother, Adeline West. Several years ago, my father's side of the family had a reunion in Oxford, Mississippi, where he grew up. While we were there, I stumbled upon several documents in my grandfather's home office — he was a history professor, too."

"Runs in the family," Matt commented.

"It's not on the scale of the Gauthiers' attorney lineage. My grandfather and I are the only professors. Anyway, many of the documents I found appeared to be written in code, but as I delved deeper into her past, I discovered that Adeline was not the typical former slave turned housewife. She was also a schoolteacher."

"So it *does* run in the family."

Tamryn smiled. "I guess you're right. But Adeline West was much more than just a schoolteacher. I believe my great-great-great-grandmother, with the help of *your* ancestor Nicolette Gauthier opened the first school for black children in the United States."

Matt didn't have the kind of reaction Tamryn was hoping for. His eyes were expressionless, his countenance completely neutral.

The tiny part of her that had hoped he would confirm her suspicions the minute she mentioned Nicolette died a swift death.

"From your lack of response, I assume there were no stories of sweet aunt Nicolette's school for slave children told around the Thanksgiving table back at the Gauthier house."

He shook his head. "Sorry." After a moment he cleared his throat and continued, "The only thing I've heard about Nicolette Gauthier is that she was a bit of a society woman. Loved to throw parties."

"Oh, there was much more to her than that. Granted, so far I haven't been able to find much written about her past, but from what little I have uncovered, it's more than obvious that she was an activist. The fact that she and Micah Gauthier hid runaway slaves in their home gives you a glimpse into the kind of people they were."

He only shrugged a shoulder.

Tamryn couldn't squelch her disappointed sigh. "I was really hoping that you would be able to confirm some of the stories that were told in *my* family around the holidays. Some believe it's just folklore, but the more I research, the more convinced I am that my great-great-great-grandmother changed the history of African-Americans in this country."

"And you think the town of Gauthier played a part?"

"Yes." She nodded. "The letters *NFG* were written in the margins of some of the documents I've uncovered. I believe those letters stand for Nicolette Fortier Gauthier. I suspect she aided Adeline in starting the school. I just haven't found the type of definitive proof that would pass muster when presenting my findings to a potential publisher. My grandfather believes that either Nicolette or Adeline kept a diary, but I haven't found any proof of that. So far, everything I've discovered is anecdotal."

"Maybe it is," he said. "Maybe it's all just circumstantial. I've never once heard anything about a school for slave children, especially the first one ever in the entire country. That's the type of stuff the Gauthier family would boast about."

Tamryn shook her head with a vehemence she couldn't curb. "It's there," she said, slapping her palm flat on the table. "I know it is. I just have to find it." She glanced at him, and heat climbed up her cheeks. "I'm sorry. As you can probably tell, I get a little passionate about this."

"Nothing wrong with showing a little passion for something you believe in," he said. A glint of humor lit his eyes. "If you're this enthusiastic when you teach, there must be a waiting list to get into your classes. I think if I'd had you for a professor I would have paid a lot more attention in freshman history."

Tamryn cursed the blush that she knew was coloring her cheeks. "You must be a very effective attorney, because you certainly talk a good game," she remarked.

"It comes in handy in more than just the courtroom," Matt quipped.

She pulled her bottom lip between her teeth to prevent the grin that was threatening to unleash itself. So much for keeping this interview professional.

The theme from the *Rocky* movies started playing from the vicinity of his chest.

"Sorry," he said, pulling his phone from the inside pocket of his suit jacket. "That's my campaign manager's special ringtone."

Matt answered the phone and immediately frowned. He lifted the sleeve of his jacket and glanced at the silver watch. "I didn't realize it was so late. I'm over at Emile's. I'll be there in ten minutes." He slid his finger across the phone's touch screen and repocketed it. "My campaign manager is waiting for me back at the office. We were supposed to leave for Baton Rouge fifteen minutes ago. I'm officially filing my intent to run today."

"Congratulations," Tamryn said. "You should have mentioned that it was such a big day for you."

He shrugged and signaled for the waiter. "Just a part of the process."

"Are you always this cool, calm and collected?"

"Another trait of a good attorney. Never let them see you sweat." He winked at her as he reached inside his jacket for his wallet, but Tamryn captured the leather folder from the waiter before he could sit it on the table. "What are you doing?" Matt asked.

"Paying for lunch. I was the one who asked for the interview," she said.

"Professor West, you're in the South." He

plucked the portfolio from her fingers, tucked a fifty-dollar bill inside and handed it to the waiter. "You do not pay for the meal. Ever."

Tamryn tipped her head to the side, as if thinking hard. "Exactly how am I *not* supposed to consider that sexist?"

"I don't care how you consider it," he said. "As long as your money never touches this table. I do have a reputation as a proper Southern gentleman to uphold."

"Well, far be it from me to trigger the demise of your reputation. I shall just say thank-you for the lunch and for finally granting me an interview."

He came around to her side of the table and pulled her chair out. Against her ear, he whispered, "Much to my surprise, it was my pleasure. I don't know why I resisted for so long."

His warm, coffee-scented breath set off a throng of flutters through her stomach.

"You Southern gentlemen lay that charm on thicker than cream cheese," Tamryn commented, rising from her seat and taking the container with her dessert.

With a chuckle, he said, "We pride ourselves on it."

He cupped her elbow and led her out of the restaurant, helping her down the steps

81

of the expansive porch that spanned the front of Emile's and the two establishments on either side of it.

Once they reached the brick sidewalk, Matt released her arm and said, "Good luck with your research, Professor. I'm sure I'll see you around town."

"Actually, you'll see me at your office. Dr. Lawrence invited me to join him and his students when they return in a couple of weeks."

Another of those lazy smiles drew across his face. "Gauthier is a small town. I'm sure I won't have to suffer through a couple of weeks without seeing you."

Tamryn slowly shook her head as she stared up at him. "Thicker than cream cheese," she said again.

His eyes glittered with amusement, his dimple winking at her as he turned and headed back toward his office building.

"You'd better watch yourself around that one," Tamryn murmured. After the beating her ego had taken courtesy of her ex-boyfriend, Reid, she was ripe for being swept off her feet by a handsome charmer with even an ounce of appeal.

"And Lord knows he's got appeal," Tamryn said.

She headed for the car Phylicia Phillips

had graciously loaned her after the rental company had been unable to deliver her another car this morning. The trusting nature of the people in this town went beyond anything Tamryn had ever experienced.

Hours later, as afternoon melted into evening, Tamryn lounged back in the wooden Adirondack chair on her room's private balcony. She'd delayed her arrival at Belle Maison by three days for the opportunity to get this room, and after only a couple of warm, relaxing hours out here, she'd concluded that it had been well worth it.

She sipped from the glass of freshly brewed ginger-peach iced tea Phylicia had insisted she try, then continued to browse through the academic journal on her electronic tablet. But there was nothing in the *Journal of Women, Politics and Policy* that could hold her attention, not when her mind was hell-bent on wandering to her lunch with Gauthier's sexiest attorney-at-law.

Just the barest glimpse of that dimple triggered a wave of disturbingly improper thoughts. She had *so* not prepared herself for the likes of Matthew Gauthier. In fact, she had been prepared for the complete opposite of what he had turned out to be. Instead of battling the mulish hard-ass she'd encountered over her many emails and phone calls, she found herself fighting an even bigger internal battle not to fall for the magnetic charm that had obviously captivated every other woman in Gauthier.

"Be smart," Tamryn warned herself in a quiet whisper.

She'd allowed stomach flutters and skin tingles to obliterate her good sense before. Her normal intelligence had the unfortunate habit of fleeing when faced with a handsome man who laid on the heavy charm. She was still tending to the scars left behind by the betrayal of the last man she'd had the misfortune of falling for, and Matthew Gauthier was ten times more handsome and charming than Reid Hayes.

She was just grateful she had several months before she would have to sit across from her ex in a faculty meeting.

Speaking of . . .

Tamryn switched to the email app on her iPad and brought up her university email. She'd emailed draft copies of the syllabi for the two classes she planned to teach next semester to the head of the History Department, Dr. Sanderson. She'd debated back and forth over whether or not to add her

Impact of Civil Rights on the Women's Liberation Movement course to this fall's classes, but Reid's repeated insistence that professors on the tenure track should spend less time in the classroom and more time conducting research had stuck with her.

He might be a lying asshole, but he was a lying asshole with tenure. He knew what it took to navigate the often-treacherous waters of academia.

Tamryn opened the email from Dr. Sanderson, but its contents were not what she had been expecting. Instead of feedback on the syllabi she'd submitted, the department head had replied with news that the scheduling of classes for the fall semester was on hold, pending a decision by Brimley's Board of Regents on possible faculty cuts that might have to be made in order to comply with recent budget constraints.

Tamryn set the electronic tablet on her thighs and tried to ignore the instant wave of unease that traveled along her spine. She was one of only a handful of professors in the entire School of Humanities who was not tenured. She didn't want to think about what it would mean for her job — for her research — if a reduction in staff were imminent.

She wouldn't think about it. She *couldn't.*

After all the work she'd put into this research, the implications of what it would mean to her career if she lost her position at Brimley were too painful to contemplate.

CHAPTER 4

Glancing once again at the directions Phylicia had given her before leaving Belle Maison, Tamryn made a left onto Cottonwood
Drive. She knew she was heading in the
right direction the moment she saw the
numerous cars parked along the tree-lined
street. Phylicia had told her to anticipate
half the town showing up for the picnic being thrown by Dr. Landry, who owned the
Gauthier Pharmacy and Feed Store on
Main Street.

Tamryn had been taken aback when she'd
walked into the store and, after only a few
minutes of chatting with the pharmacist and
cashier, had been invited to the gathering.
Although she shouldn't have been all that
surprised. In the week since she'd arrived in
Gauthier, she had already received an
invitation to Sunday dinner from the
beauty-parlor owner, Claudette Robinson,
and to a baby shower from a woman whose

name she couldn't recall.

She pulled in behind a blue pickup truck and locked up the compact sedan the rental-car company had finally delivered to Belle Maison. It was smaller than the car she'd originally rented, but Tamryn feared she'd be without a car for another several days if she demanded they replace it.

She locked the car, chuckling at the fact that, in this town, that was more than likely unnecessary, and followed the sounds of music and children's laughter coming from a huge white colonial several houses down the street. She walked past the cars lining the driveway and headed for the gate that led to the backyard. She smoothed her hands down the sides of her flowing yellow-and-blue-striped maxi dress before pushing open the gate and slipping inside.

The party was in full swing. There were at least a dozen tables set up around the massive fenced-in yard, all occupied by people feasting on the barbecue that she'd smelled halfway down the street. Smoke billowed from a large barrel-style grill over on the left side of the yard. Next to it was another table, this one covered with chafing dishes, platters and huge bowls. Next to that was a
—Was that a rowboat?

"Well, look who's here. It's the professor!"

Tamryn was approached by one of the women she'd met at Claudette's the other day, Mabel something or other. "Well, don't just stand there," the woman said. "Come on in and get yourself something to eat. You look like you can use it. It's been forty years since I was able to get into a dress that small."

She was immediately surrounded by a host of people eager to greet the newest guest. Despite not having met the majority of them during her brief visits to downtown Gauthier, everyone who introduced themselves seem to already know her name, that she was a professor "at a fancy school up North" and that she was visiting Gauthier because of the discovery at the law firm.

As they approached the food tables, two men carrying a large pot stepped up to the rowboat and emptied a heap of steaming mudbugs into it. Tamryn had only encountered the shellfish when she visited her father's family in Mississippi. She'd never been able to bring herself to eat one.

As they made their way along the buffet, Mabel kept up her chatter. "Isn't that something about the room they found at the Gauthier Law Firm?" she said as she heaped a dollop of potato salad onto Tamryn's already crowded plate. "You know, my grandmother used to say that Ansel — that was Micah and Nicolette's son — married a slave girl. I think he must have been helping her escape and they fell in love. Doesn't that sound romantic?"

"Yes, it does," Tamryn said. "I wouldn't be surprised if that's exactly how it happened. I've run across stories like that many times during my research. If you don't mind, I'd love to interview you about some of the other things your grandmother might have mentioned."

Mabel's eyes widened with delight at the thought of being interviewed. Tamryn figured she'd have to dedicate an entire day for it. The woman was a talker.

After they made their way out of the buffet line, Tamryn was invited to one of the tables and was introduced to yet another group of residents. They regaled her with stories of Gauthier's economic boom since the Underground Railroad discovery, and how the flood of new tourists had revived the town.

A group of teens came to the table with plates in their hands, looking for a place to sit. Tamryn gave up her spot and walked over to the other side of the yard, settling on a wooden tree swing built for two that provided the perfect view of a serious game of kickball in progress. She laughed at the chubby toddlers who missed the ball more than they struck it.

Not for the first time since she'd arrived, a sense of peace stole over her. There was just something about this town's easy nature that called to her.

She pushed off the ground using the tips of her toes and set the swing on a gentle sway. She'd been relaxing for a few minutes when she felt a prickle of awareness cascade down her spine.

Tamryn looked to her left and spotted Matthew Gauthier striding toward her with a confident, easy smile gracing his lips. He wore jeans and a T-shirt, looking more like the biker she'd encountered her first day in Gauthier than the lawyer. He carried a flat brown cardboard tray, like the ones used to store canned soft drinks in the grocery store.

"Hello there," Tamryn said as he approached.

"Hello," he said, settling next to her on the swing without even asking if he could join her.

She pointed to the cardboard tray, which was piled high with mudbugs. "Think you got enough mudbugs there?"

"Around here we call them crawfish, not mudbugs. And this is just my first round.

When Errol Landry is doing the boiling, you want to eat as many as you can. He makes a special trip back to Gauthier every year for his dad's picnic, just so he can boil the crawfish."

"So is that the reason for the party? A homecoming celebration for Dr. Landry's son?"

Matt shook his head as he ripped the tail off the crustacean and wrapped his lips around the body, sucking it. Tamryn wasn't sure whether to laugh or gag.

"Doc Landry throws this picnic every year just as a thank-you to the community. It's not as if folks wouldn't support his business — Gauthier is lucky to have him. Still —" Matt shrugged "— it's his way of showing his appreciation."

Warmth settled in Tamryn's chest. "I absolutely adore this town," she said.

He looked over at her, his brow lifted in a skeptical hitch. "Because the local pharmacist invited you to his yearly picnic that's open to everyone in town?"

"That's not the only reason. Everyone is just so warm and inviting here. I've only been in Gauthier a week, but you wouldn't know it by the way I've been treated. The people here have gone out of their way to make me feel at home."

He looked over at her and grinned. "I hate to burst your bubble, but they're only doing that because they're nosy and you're the shiny, new attraction in town."

Tamryn's head flew back. "Thanks for putting my ego in check."

Her crack of laughter drew particularly interested stares from the group of ladies she'd spoken to earlier. They all looked toward her and Matt with approving smiles on their faces.

"We seem to be the object of quite a few stares," Tamryn observed.

Matt looked over to the table and waved. "Told you," he said. "Nosy as hell."

"Stop it. They've all been very sweet to me."

His lazy gaze traveled the length of her body before settling on her lips. "I'm finding that being sweet toward you is not hard to do."

"Thank you," she said with a demure smile.

Matthew's eyes remained on her lips for several heated moments more before he seemed to shake himself out of a daze and returned to his carton of crawfish. He peeled off another and sucked it.

Tamryn couldn't hold it in. She burst out laughing.

"What?" Matt asked.

"I can't believe you're sucking on that."

"Because that's where all the flavor is." He held one out to her. "Here, give it a try."

She put a hand up. "I'll pass."

"Come on. You cannot come to Louisiana during crawfish season and not suck at least one head." His eyes flew to hers. "It only sounds sexual. Don't slap me for talking dirty." He shoved the crawfish toward her again. "Go on, give it a try."

She shook her head.

"Well, at least try the tail."

Tamryn eyed the little curl of meat and, after a bit of hesitation, leaned over and captured the piece Matt held out to her between her teeth.

"Mmm . . ." she murmured. "Good." She coughed and tapped her chest. "Spicy."

Matt's eyes remained on her mouth. He watched her for several moments, his eyes intense as he stared at her. The heat that traveled along her skin had nothing to do with the spicy food she'd just consumed.

Without taking his eyes off her mouth, Matt peeled another crawfish tail and held it up to her. "Another?" he asked.

Tamryn nodded, once again eating from his fingers.

Matt released an audible breath. He

dropped the other half of the crawfish into the box and picked up the longneck beer he'd carried with him.

Tamryn nodded toward the crawfish head he'd tossed on top of the others. "You're not going to suck it?"

He shook his head. "This time it *would* be sexual."

Her head fell back with another peal of laughter that again drew stares.

"That sexy laugh isn't helping," Matt said. He blew out a deep breath and twisted around on the swing. "We need to talk about something else. How's the research going?"

"You don't find talk of historic research stimulating?"

"Not as stimulating as talk of sucking heads," he said with another swig of beer.

Tamryn wasn't sure she agreed. Just having him near her inspired all sorts of stimulating thoughts. Especially in those jeans he wore.

"So?" he asked. "Made any breakthroughs with the research?"

"Unfortunately, I haven't found anything new relating to the connection between Nicolette Gauthier and Adeline West," she said. "But then again, I haven't started the really intense research yet. That'll happen in a couple of days, when I start working in the archives at Xavier University. They have an extensive collection on African-American history specific to Louisiana." Tamryn rubbed her hands together. "I can't wait."

Matt stared at her as if she was an alien with six arms.

"I have never in my life seen someone so excited about visiting a library," he said, shaking his head. He pulled out his phone. "What's your cell number? I know the head of the History Department at Xavier. I can put you in contact with him."

Tamryn gasped. "Dr. Ezekiel Marsh?"

"Yeah, you know him?"

"I don't *know* him know him, but I know of him, of course. I use his textbook on the African diaspora in several of my classes. He's renowned in my circle."

"Well, in my circle, he's a frat brother who made me eat cat food when I pledged to my fraternity. Thankfully, he's outgrown such nonsense."

Tamryn choked on a laugh. "You don't seem like the frat-boy type."

He shrugged. "Another of those family things. All the men in my family pledged to the same fraternity. It's what was expected."

She tipped her head to the side, studying his strong profile. "So, do you always do what's expected of you?"

"Not always," he said. "I've been known to occasionally break with tradition and do my own thing."

Her brow arched. "Like driving a motor-cycle?"

"Yes, as far as I know, I'm the only Gauthier man to drive a Ducati." His eyes creased at the corners as a sly grin broke out across his face. "Whenever you're ready for another ride, just say the word. I usually prefer riding solo, but I have to admit that I enjoyed seeing you straddle my bike."

The breath she was just about to take clogged in her lungs. Must his voice sound so sexy?

"I have a feeling letting you take me for a ride would be dangerous," Tamryn replied.

That grin hitched a bit higher as his hooded gaze zeroed in on her mouth. "I can promise it would be worth it."

Her stomach quivered. The husky timbre of his voice, combined with those entrancing dimples and mesmerizing green-and-hazel eyes, posed all kinds of threats to her resolve to remain focused on her work. If she was not careful, she could find herself losing sight of her goal, something she refused to let happen again. It had cost her too much the first time.

"I'm afraid I'll have to decline your offer," Tamryn said. She would not allow the flash of disappointment that shadowed his face to affect her. She pushed up from the swing. "Thanks for the introduction to yet another Louisiana delicacy."

"It was my pleasure," he said as he rose. "Are you leaving?"

She nodded. "I have a lot of work to do tonight."

"Let me walk you to your car."

"No, I can manage."

He slanted her a look. "You remember that Southern-gentleman thing I mentioned the other day, right? I can't allow you to walk to your car alone, especially with all the eyes watching us. I'd never hear the end of it."

"Ah, yes. The reputation. It must remain intact." She shook her head. "It must be exhausting trying to live up to the standards of being a Southern gentleman."

"Only when the tasks are unpleasant," he said. "And I think we both know that isn't the case this time."

He crooked his arm, an invitation for her to thread hers through it. When she obliged, Tamryn was sure she heard a collective sigh of approval coming from the ladies who had been watching them earlier. As she walked alongside him, her body gave its own appreciative sigh, relaxing into their easy stroll.

Matt might not think he posed a danger to her, but Tamryn was under no illusions. With very little effort, this man had the potential to sidetrack her from all of her well-laid plans.

They arrived at her car and he opened the door for her, but instead of moving to the side so that she could get in, he stood inside the doorway, draping his arm on the door.

"Let me take you to dinner tonight," he said.

Tamryn was astounded at how quickly she almost agreed. Even though a mental list of all the reasons why getting involved with Matthew Gauthier was a bad idea ran on a constant loop inside her head, the urge to say yes to his invitation was so strong that it pained her when she said, "I really cannot, Matt."

"Why?"

Folding her arms over her chest, she said, "Maybe I should be asking you that question."

His head reared back slightly. "What question? *Why I asked you to dinner?*"

"Yes."

"What kind of question is that?"

"A legitimate one," she said. "You've spent

the past six months avoiding me. Why this sudden desire to take me to dinner?"

He blew out a ragged breath and ran both hands down his face. He glanced over at the house across the street and then brought his eyes back to her.

"Here's the thing," he started, holding his hands up. "If I come right out and admit that it's because I think you're one of the hottest women I've ever met, it will make me sound shallow."

Tamryn pulled her bottom lip between her teeth. "That does come across as a bit shallow —"

"You see —"

"— but honest," she continued. "I appreciate honesty."

His gaze narrowed as he closed the car door and leaned against it. "You want honest?" he asked. "Because if you want me to be completely honest, I can admit that when it comes to you, this whole Southern-gentleman thing is just an act. There is nothing even remotely gentleman-like that runs across my mind when I look at you."

Her breath faltered as it crawled from her lungs. She coughed to clear away the desire that had lodged in her throat. "Well, I asked for honest, didn't I?" Tamryn said.

Matt closed the distance between them.

He reached down and captured her left hand. He trailed the fingers of his right hand down her cheek, letting them linger on her jaw.

"Just dinner," he said. "We can start there."

Tamryn shut her eyes tight against the powerful yearning that surged inside of her. Then she thought about the blows her career had already sustained after the last time she allowed her emotions to get in the way of her common sense.

"I can't," she said. She took a step back, then went around him and got into her rental car. She didn't even chance looking at him out the driver's side window. She started the car and pulled away from the curb before she lost all ability to fight the lust that threatened to get her in a heap of trouble she didn't need this summer.

CHAPTER 5

Matt's knee bounced in tandem with the nervous rhythm he struck on his desk with his pen. He eyed his phone, debating the wisdom of pressing the second button from the top.

Unable to fight the urge, he jabbed at the desk phone, buzzing Carmen's extension.

"What about the tent company?" he asked. "They know we need two tents, right?"

"Look out your window. They're erecting the second tent right now."

He jumped out of his chair and rushed over to the window. Sure enough, a blue-and-white-striped canopy extended across a twenty-by-thirty-five-foot portion of Heritage Park. He noticed a stack of metal poles lying where the other tent was to be erected. A portable stage had been constructed earlier this morning and was now being adorned with royal-blue-and-white silk bunting, the campaign colors Ben had chosen because blue represented power and integrity.

Matt returned to his desk, a small portion of his anxiety appeased now that things were falling into place. It had all become official early last week when he'd filed his statement of candidacy papers at the state-capitol building in Baton Rouge, but it wasn't until this morning — the day of his official campaign kickoff rally — that it had truly sunk in.

He was in this. There was no turning back now.

Today's rally was just the start of what would be several weeks of intense campaigning, all leading up to a special election to fill the prematurely vacated District Twelve senate seat. The crowd at this evening's rally would tell Matt a lot in terms of how much support he could expect from the citizens in and around this area.

He buzzed Carmen again. "What about the cotton candy and popcorn machines? The vendor knows he needs to be here at least an hour before the rally starts, right?" His question was met with silence from the other end of the line. "Carmen?"

His office door swung open.

"Matt, get out of here right now," Carmen yelled.

He put his hands up in surrender. "I'm just trying to make sure everything is in place."

Carmen plopped her hands on her hips. "When was the last time the electricity here was cut off, or the office supplies not delivered or the bathroom out of toilet paper?" she snarled. "You don't have to worry about any of that because I get all that done. That's my job. Now, get out of this office before you drive me crazy and I'm forced to kill you."

Matt figured she was only half-joking. "Fine," he said, rising from behind his desk. "Maybe a walk will help me settle down."

"Do not step foot in Heritage Park," Carmen warned. "The people setting up over there don't need you bugging them."

"Am I allowed to walk over to Shayla's place for a latte?" he asked as he followed Carmen out of his office.

"Only if you make it decaf. Caffeine is the last thing you need right now."

She shot him another nasty look as she sat back at her desk.

"Matt?" Carmen called just as he grabbed the door handle. He turned. "You don't have anything to be nervous about," she said, her voice void of its previous bite. "Patrick Carter might be a lifelong politician, but you're a lifelong Gauthier. The people in this town already know who the best candidate is."

"Thanks," he said with a lopsided grin. Carmen always knew just what to say to settle him down. He would probably have driven this law firm into the ground a long time ago if she wasn't here to keep it running. "You want me to bring you something back from Shayla's?"

She waved off his offer. "That place is dangerous. You go in there for an innocent cup of coffee and come out with a muffin the size of your head and a thousand-calorie extra-large mocha chai latte something or other."

"With extra whipped cream," Matt added with a wink, closing the door behind him.

He headed left down Main Street, looking up into the cloudless, picture-perfect blue sky. Maybe he should look at the beautiful weather as a sign of things to come. How could he bomb at his rally on such a gorgeous day?

A smile drew across his face as he came upon the iron round tables and chairs set up in front of The Jazzy Bean, the new coffee shop that had just opened in the Main Street storefront once occupied by Armant's Antiques Shop.

"We meet again," Matt said in greeting.

Tamryn looked up from the yellow legal pad she'd been scribbling on. Matt took full ownership of the immense rush of pleasure he experienced at the sight of her broad, surprised smile.

"Well, good morning," she said.

He nodded toward the table's other empty chair. "Do you mind?"

She gestured for him to take a seat. "Be my guest."

As he sat, Matt eyed the collection of items spread across the table. There were two legal pads, several blocks of colorful sticky notes and an iPad.

"This looks intense," he remarked.

She expelled a sigh and tossed her pen on the table. "*Intense* is one way to describe it. *Frustrating, nerve-racking.* Take your pick of adjectives."

"You mean all of my wonderful answers to your questions at lunch last week didn't help?"

"You did," she said with a grin. "Unfortunately, there are still huge holes in my grandmother's past, and I just can't find what I'm looking for." She huffed out a humorless laugh. "It would help if I knew exactly *what* I was looking for and if it actually exists. Is it the diary my grandfather

106

talked about? Is there something else?" She ran a frustrated hand through her wavy hair. "Maybe it all really is the stuff of legends."

She looked over at him, her eyes teeming with raw anguish. "If I have to return to Brimley without evidence of the slave school's beginnings, I'm not sure if I'll be able to face my colleagues. So many of them told me I was wasting my time chasing this."

The jolt of guilt that sliced through Matt was powerful enough to cause a physical ache in his chest. The story she was chasing wasn't just the stuff of legends. He'd held the proof in his hands.

Last night, he'd gone into his family's library and pulled out the worn leather-bound diary that had resided in the confines of the hidden wall safe for generations. Within its yellowed, brittle pages were the words of his great-great-aunt, Nicolette Gauthier. It contained a detailed account of the school she and a woman by the name of Adeline Marchand had created. Matt had no doubts that Adeline Marchand was Adeline West.

If only the diary wasn't also filled with page after page of the horrible acts his family had committed against this town during its earliest days. If only the Gauthier family had not gone on to commit so many *more* transgressions against the town — transgressions that, if ever brought to light, would be used by his opponent to tear him apart in a political campaign.

For the briefest moment last night, he'd considered setting the diary on fire so that he could finally be free of the secrets it held, but he couldn't bring himself to do it. One of the promises he'd made to his mother was that he would preserve the Gauthier family's historical artifacts. Why she wanted to do anything for a family that had caused her such grief was beyond him, but Matt could not bring himself to go against one of his mother's dying wishes.

Matt stared at the exasperation on Tamryn's face and his guilt tripled. At the moment he hated himself, knowing he possessed the information she needed, yet unable to share it with her. The risk to his future plans was just too great.

"I'm sorry I couldn't be much help," Matt said. "To make up for it, how about I give you the official tour of downtown Gauthier? I can point out the structures and share what I know about their history. Although I should warn you that I don't know nearly as much as I probably should, seeing as I've lived here my entire life. Like I said before, history isn't my thing."

She lifted the insulated paper cup to her lips and sipped from it. "You actually have time in your busy schedule to spend the afternoon showing me around Gauthier?"

"When you're the boss you can get away with just about anything." He winked, then a wry grin curled up the corners of his lips. "And Carmen threatened to kill me if I hung around the office a second longer. I have my official campaign kickoff rally tonight, and it turns out that I'm a bit more nervous than I thought I would be. I figure if I want to keep her as my office manager, it's best that I get out of her hair for a few hours."

A knowing glint entered Tamryn's eyes. "So this date is really more about saving your hide than sharing the history of downtown Gauthier." Her eyes widened with a look of horror. "I didn't mean 'date' as in a *date* date."

God, she was beautiful when she was flustered. Matt leaned across the table and whispered, "But I want you to mean 'date' as in a *date* date. My offer to take you out to dinner still stands."

The crests of her pronounced cheeks flushed red. It was so easy to make her blush.

"You do realize that I'm in Gauthier to

work, don't you?" Tamryn asked.

Yes, he did. But the more he kept her from doing that work, the less likely she was to run across something that could erupt in a scandal that could end his political career before it fully got off the ground.

"That's not an excuse. You can't work 24/7," he said. "However, you are right about this particular outing. This is definitely not a *date* date. When I convince you to join me on a real date, you'll understand the difference."

Tamryn settled back in her chair and folded her arms across her chest. "The list must be a mile long," she murmured.

Matt hitched a brow. "The list?"

"Of all the poor hearts you've left broken around Gauthier."

"I'm not in the business of breaking hearts, Professor West."

"Go tell that to the ladies in Claudette's."

They were interrupted by Shayla Kirkland, owner of The Jazzy Bean Coffee Shop.

"How's it going, Matt?" Shayla asked. "Today's the big day, huh?"

"Yes, it is," Matt said, standing to give her a hug. He'd played basketball with Shayla's brother, Braylon, back in high school. Braylon had died a few months ago, just after returning from a tour in Afghanistan, and

110

now Shayla was helping her sister-in-law raise his two young daughters.

"Can I get you anything?" she asked.

He pointed to Tamryn's cup. "What's in there?"

"Earl Grey tea. No sugar," Tamryn answered.

Matt's face scrunched up in a frown. "I don't think so. Get me one of those thousand-calorie concoctions, with extra shots and double pumps and whipped cream drizzling down the side of the cup."

"You got it," Shayla said.

Tamryn shook her head, a huge grin creasing her face. "Aren't you supposed to be in training to run a 5K? Is a thousand-calorie coffee drink a part of your regimen?"

"Am I getting it wrong?"

"I think so."

"Maybe you should step in as my trainer. There's a running path along the wooded area around Belle Maison. I think we should start running together so that we'll be ready for the 5K."

"And you called *me* persistent?"

Matt laughed. "You were." He folded his arms on the table and leaned forward. "But I'm a lot more persistent than you are, especially when it comes to something I really want."

"And what is it that you want?" she asked.

"A date. Several dates. Anything you're willing to offer, as long as it includes getting to know you better."

Before Tamryn could answer, Shayla returned with his drink. Matt handed her a ten-dollar bill and told her to put the change in the tip jar.

He returned his attention to Tamryn, but Matt couldn't decipher the expression on her face. His heart thumped in his chest as he awaited her answer. In that moment, he realized that as much as he wanted to keep her away from her work, the desire to satisfy his curiosity about her was just as great.

It was the combination of intelligence, outrageous beauty and that hint of sass that peeked out; it had him practically salivating at the chance to get to know her better.

She flipped over the pages on the legal pad she'd been scribbling on and reached for the red leather messenger bag that she'd taken from her car when he'd first found her stranded the day she arrived in Gauthier.

"I'll take you up on the tour you offered," she said, stuffing the tablet, along with the rest of the items, into her bag.

"What about my other offer?"

She averted her eyes, staring across the

street. When she brought them back to his, they held a note of apology. "I'm not ready for a *date* date just yet." Regret and just a hint of sadness drew across her face. "You're so different than I thought you would be, Matt, and I'll probably kick myself for turning you down, but I just . . . I can't right now. I came here for a specific purpose, and if I allow myself to get sidetracked again, I'll never get this book done. I hope you understand."

He held her gaze for several long moments. "I guess I don't really have a choice," he replied. "As long as you understand that I'm not giving up."

A grin curled up the edges of her lips. "Why am I not surprised?"

The urge to lean over and taste that smile was so strong that Matt had to push himself away from the table before he caved to the impulse. He stood and took hold of the messenger bag, pulling the strap across his body. Then he picked up his coffee and motioned for Tamryn to join him.

The Jazzy Bean occupied the southernmost building along Main Street's commercial area. As they made their way up the street, Matt pointed out the various retail shops. He told her about the businesses that occupied the buildings and how all had taken on new life after last year's Underground Railroad discovery put Gauthier on the map and made it a tourist destination for history buffs.

"It's good to see the boost businesses have received. There aren't many places like Main Street left around here," Matt commented.

"Or anywhere," Tamryn said. "I'd argue that this place was a national treasure even before the discovery in your law office. It's like stepping back in time."

"The shop owners go to great pains to preserve the storefronts on Main Street. We all signed a pledge promising to keep up our end of the bargain so that Main Street will look the same for generations to come."

Tamryn wrapped her arms around herself. "Being a city girl, I have very little experience with a town this small, a community this close-knit. It must have been great growing up here."

A disgruntled snort escaped him before he had the chance to curb it.

She looked over at him. "It wasn't?"

"It had its pluses and minuses," Matt said with a shrug. "Remember when you asked me if there were privileges or obligations to being a Gauthier?" She nodded. "There were many more of the latter. If you carried the Gauthier name, there were certain expectations that you were expected to fulfill."

Matt pointed across the street to the Gauthier Law Firm.

"My first memory is of walking through the doors of that building when I was three years old. I remember my grandfather picking me up and sitting me on top of his desk. He told me it was going to be my desk someday."

"And it is," she mused.

"Still has the smiley face I drew on the very bottom drawer with permanent marker," he admitted. "I never even thought about being anything but a lawyer or about practicing anywhere but here in Gauthier. My path was laid out for me a long time ago."

"So you never considered anything else? Even when the rest of your sixth-grade classmates wanted to be firemen, or astronauts, or . . ." She paused, tilted her head to the side. "What other things do sixth-grade boys want to be?"

"I don't know," Matt said with a laugh. "Like I said, I've known since I was three years old that I was going to be a lawyer."

"Do you resent it, having your career path laid out for you from such an early age?"

"I used to," he said. "But then again, I don't know what else I would have done with my life. I never had the chance to contemplate anything else." He looked over at her. "Have you always wanted to be a professor?"

"Oh, no." She shook her head. "I wanted to be a disc jockey."

A burst of shocked laughter rushed from his mouth. He hadn't been expecting that one. "A disc jockey?"

"Yep. When I was younger, I would sit in my bedroom for hours listening to the radio. The disc jockey used to interview all of these celebrities. I was so jealous. It wasn't until I was much older that I discovered the celebrities were rarely in the studio. They were mostly call-ins."

He held her hand as they crossed the street in front of the dry cleaner's.

"So how does a wannabe disc jockey become a history professor?" Matt asked.

"A visit to my great-grandmother's the summer before my freshman year of high school." She looked over at him, a wistful smile on her lips. "That summer, my great-grandmother told me about *her* grand-mother, Adeline West. I was completely enthralled. I tried to learn all I could about her, which wasn't easy, being that internet access was very sparse back then.

"As I researched Adeline's past, I found myself falling more and more in love with history in general. I ran across so many fascinating women of color who have never made it into the history books."

"So you decided to write your own."

"Yes." She nodded. "I felt they needed a voice." She nudged his arm. "And that was a nice try, but we weren't done talking about you."

"We weren't?"

She shook her head. "I want to know about your move to politics. Was that ordained, too?"

"Nah." Matt shook his head. "Not every Gauthier man has gone into politics." He gestured to his law office. "My grandfather worked in that building over there until his cardiologist forced him to retire. And my uncle Cleveland, he was never bitten by the politics bug. Although he died of cancer in his early fifties, so he might have run for office if he'd been here long enough."

"What made you decide to run?"

"Hey, I thought the purpose of this tour was for you to learn more about Gauthier, the town?"

"It is, but I'm finding talk of this Gauthier man equally as fascinating."

"Well, that's encouraging," Matt said with a sly grin. "You know, if we went on a *date* date, you'd learn even more."

Tamryn rolled her eyes.

They entered Heritage Park through the front entrance, walking under the vine-covered arch that curved across the brick-laid walkway. Tamryn headed for the activity on the right side of the park, where the tents and stage were being set up, but Matt caught her arm.

"Not that way," he said. "That's in Carmen's Do Not Enter territory. I was threatened with bodily harm if I'm caught pestering the workers."

Tamryn's head flew back with a laugh. "I'm starting to suspect that you're a bit intimidated by your office manager."

"I'm terrified of my office manager," he said. "Terrified that I'll lose her, that is. I do whatever it takes to make her happy." He tugged her wrist. "Why don't we go this way? The flowers along the arbor are in bloom. This is probably the best time of the year to visit Heritage Park."

They traveled in the opposite direction. The noise from the rally setup steadily decreased as they ventured to the other side of the park.

Matt watched Tamryn as she walked along

the path of towering oak trees, their arching branches bending to the will of the breeze. She trailed her fingers along the petals of the bright pink azaleas. When she turned and looked at him over her shoulder — a slight, sexy smile tilting her lips — Matt's breath stuttered out of his lungs.

Lord, she was beautiful. Her thick black hair fell in soft waves around her shoulders, which were left bare due to the lightweight halter-style dress she wore. The colorful material flowed all the way down to her ankles, but despite the fact that so much skin was covered up, it was still one of the sexiest looks he'd ever seen on a woman. Matt walked toward her, staying a few steps behind so that he could study the way her hips swayed as she walked.

"This is beautiful," she said, cupping a camellia in her fingers.

"I agree," he said, his eyes trained on her. "Beautiful."

Her soft brown cheeks reddened. "You really do have that charming—Southern-gentleman thing down to a science, you know that?"

"Some people make it very easy," he said. "But I already told you that being a Southern gentleman is far from my mind when I'm around you."

She stepped up to him, stopping about a foot in front of him. Her eyes locked with his, amusement gleaming within their warm, brown depths. "Do I really inspire ungentlemanly thoughts in you?"

"You have no idea," Matt pushed out with an uneasy breath.

"I have a hard time believing this charming guy is the same person who spent so much of the past six months dodging me."

"I'm starting to regret that," he said.

"You are, huh?"

"Oh, yeah." Matt nodded. "It puts me at a disadvantage. I fear I'm having to work a lot harder than I would have if only I had been more . . . accommodating."

"And what is it exactly that you're working toward again?"

He stepped up to her, so close he could smell her soft lavender scent. "I doubt it's hard for that brilliant mind of yours to figure out what it is I want."

As he'd anticipated, those cheeks became even redder. God, she was gorgeous.

"Now I see how you've been driving the single women of Gauthier crazy," Tamryn said.

"Not true," he returned. "But now I'm curious. What is it about me that you think would be so appealing to the single women of Gauthier?"

"Those dimples alone are enough to drive a woman crazy," she said.

"Dimples? Really? That's all it takes?"

"For some, yes. All it takes are killer dimples."

"Are you one of those women who falls for a man with dimples?"

The hint of naughtiness gleaming in her chocolate-brown eyes sent a delicious ripple down Matt's spine.

"I don't know if that's something I'm ready to reveal just yet," she said before turning and continuing on the path.

"No, no, no." He caught her hand and pulled her toward him. "You don't get to leave until you answer the question."

"Says who?"

He didn't reply. He didn't let go of her hand, either.

"You're used to getting your way, aren't you?" Tamryn asked.

He shrugged. "I'm an only child. It comes with the territory." He pulled her closer. "Now, tell me. How much will flashing my dimples help with my campaign?"

"I'm sure those dimples will win you a lot of votes."

Matt dipped his head until his forehead nearly touched hers. In a low murmur, he said, "I think you know that's not the campaign I'm talking about."

The urge to kiss her was so potent, so dangerously powerful that Matt had to remind himself it wasn't his God-given right. At the moment, he couldn't think of anything but giving into the impulse to discover how her mouth would feel against his.

"Why are you making this so difficult?" she asked in a breathless whisper.

"What am I making difficult this time?"

"The oath I took to keep things strictly professional with you."

"You took an actual oath?" He chuckled. "Did you put your hand over your heart and everything?"

"I'm being serious, Matt. The work I'm doing here in Gauthier is crucial to my career. In fact, I recently discovered that it's even more crucial than I first thought." She looked up at him. "I can't have any distractions."

"Crucial to your career? That sounds serious."

She shook her head. "It's nothing. Just work issues. But it brought home the fact that I need to concentrate on what I came to Gauthier to do. You and your dimples are a distraction I cannot afford at the moment."

"Is there something I can do to help?" Matt asked.

A pang of guilt ricocheted through him, because he knew damn well there was one thing he could do to help her. But sharing Aunt Nicolette's diary was off the table.

"I just need to remain focused," Tamryn said.

Matt snagged her hand again. He pulled it up his chest and covered it with his own. "I think you can get your work done and still give me the time of day, but I won't push you too hard. Yet."

His phone let out a loud beep. Matt pulled it from his pocket and looked at the reminder that had popped up on the screen.

"I have to practice my speech for this evening," he said, pocketing the phone. "You're staying for the rally?"

"Seems it's the place to be in Gauthier tonight."

"That's because there's not much else happening in Gauthier." He tugged her hand. "Come on. I'll walk you back to Shayla's."

"Actually, I'm going to hang around here a little longer." She pointed toward the rear of the park. "I want to check out the gazebo."

"Then I'll see you in a few hours. I'm sure you'll have your vote-for-Matt button prominently displayed, right?"

"Front and center," she said with a laugh. "Hey," Tamryn called as he headed back toward the opposite side of the park. She pointed to the messenger bag he still carried. "My bag."

Matt patted the soft leather. "I'm going to keep this until after the rally. That way I know I'll get to see you before you leave." He winked and continued walking.

Tamryn leaned against the rough bark of a massive oak tree, marveling at the crowd gathered for Matt's rally. There were men, women and children of all ages. Mothers pushed strollers with chubby-faced babies; fathers pulled toddler-filled red Radio Flyer wagons. Teens loitered around the wooden waterwheel that seemed to be the centerpiece of the park.

There were two canopy tents set up on either side of the path that led to the stage. One tent housed a table filled with campaign paraphernalia: buttons, yard signs and bumper stickers. The other tent, manned by several of the women she'd met at Claudette's Beauty Parlor and Dr. Landry's picnic, was the place to be if you wanted a bite to eat. There were hot dogs, nachos, cotton candy and snow cones — though Tamryn had been informed that they were called snowballs around here. It was like a carnival.

Several members of Gauthier's civic association had taken to the stage to expound on the improvements that had been made in Gauthier in the past year, but they warned that there was still much that needed to be done. Now it was Matt's turn. Benjamin Keller, who had introduced himself as Matt's campaign manager, rattled off a list of Matt's academic and career accomplishments, along with his outstanding commitment to the people of Gauthier.

"Without further ado," Ben said, "may I introduce to you the future state senator of District Twelve, Matthew Ellison Gauthier."

The crowd erupted in cheers as Matt walked onto the stage. Tamryn was once again rendered breathless as she stared at him in his tailored suit. She was pretty sure she heard a collective feminine sigh when he stepped up to the microphone and flashed a smile. Those dimples should be declared lethal weapons.

"Good evening," Matt started. "There's

no big secret as to why we're gathered here this evening. You all know that I've been contemplating a run against Patrick Carter to represent the people of District Twelve in the Louisiana State legislature. With the support of numerous people from this great part of the state, I come before you all today to officially announce my candidacy."

The roar from the crowd was infectious. Tamryn couldn't help getting caught up in the celebratory mood that permeated the entire park.

Matt spoke for several more minutes, listing the goals he hoped to accomplish once he became a state senator. The only thing that wasn't met with enthusiasm was his mention of finding a way to heal the fracture between the towns of Gauthier and Maplesville. Tamryn had heard from several residents over the past couple of weeks about the tension between the neighboring towns.

Matt ended his speech to yet another roar from the crowd. Tamryn watched him as he climbed down the steps of the makeshift stage and began to greet his constituents. He shook hands and accepted congratulatory pats on the back, flashing that killer smile the entire time. He looked over to where she stood and his smile broadened.

Her belly experienced an involuntary

tremble.

Matt continued to greet folks as he made his way toward her. As he approached, Tamryn noticed that his smile had taken on a slightly more intimate tone.

"I don't think I've ever seen so much gushing over a single person," she said. "I think I might be just a bit jealous over all the attention that's being showered upon you."

Matt leaned in and whispered close to her ear, "There's only one person's attention that I care about right now."

She tilted her head toward the refreshment table, where Claudette and several of Gauthier's longtime residents stared blatantly at them. "Are you trying to start a scandal on the first official day of your candidacy?"

"The gossip about us started the morning you walked into my law office," he said. "We might as well give them something to talk about."

"I don't want to be accused of monopolizing all of Gauthier's most eligible bachelor's time."

"Too late. You already occupy much of my waking hours," he said. He leaned forward again, but was interrupted by Ben calling his name and waving him over to a group of business owners from nearby Maplesville who had showed up for the event.

"Your constituency awaits," Tamryn said.

"Will you be here for a while?"

"I do still have to get my bag from you," she said.

"That's right," he said with a laugh. He leaned forward again and whispered, "Meet me in my office in an hour."

"Are you really going to hold my bag hostage?"

His brows arched in amusement. "One hour."

Tamryn shook her head, a rueful grin edging up the corner of her mouth as she watched him confidently stride toward the group of businessmen.

She walked around the grounds of the park, chatting with the people she'd met over the course of her first week in Gauthier and answering the questions of many who seemed highly curious about the town's newest visitor.

She was browsing over the sign-up sheet for people to participate in the 5K Matt was sponsoring when she heard, "So, how are you liking Gauthier?"

Tamryn looked up to find a woman holding a baby.

"I'm Mya," the woman said. "We haven't

had a chance to meet." She wiggled the pinky finger of the hand that cradled the baby's bottom.

"Hi," Tamryn said with a laugh, giving her a pinky shake. "Tamryn West. And who is this?" She tickled the baby's pudgy chin.

"This is Kamri Alexis," she answered, smiling down at the baby, whose thick, jet-black hair was downright enviable.

"She's adorable."

"Thank you." She kissed the baby's head. "Phil tells me that you're here doing research. Don't think we were gossiping about you. This is a small town," Mya explained. "You can't break a nail without someone discussing it over a glass of sweet tea."

"It's okay." Tamryn waved off her concerned look. "And, yes, I am here doing research. I'm a history professor at Brimley College in Boston. I've been following the discovery of the stop on the Underground Railroad at the Gauthier Law Firm." Tamryn stopped short as the woman's name registered. "Wait a minute. Are you Mya Dubois-Anderson? The one who made the discovery?"

"Yes." The woman smiled. "It was my husband, Corey, and I who uncovered it."

"I would love to interview you while I'm here. I've talked to Dr. Lawrence, but there's a lot more that I want to know that maybe you can help with."

"Of course," Mya said. "How long will you be in Gauthier?"

"Until the end of July," Tamryn answered. "I'll be spending a large portion of my time between the libraries of Tulane and Xavier Universities, but maybe we can schedule something for the weekend?"

"Or even in the evenings," Mya said. "I sometimes drop in at Belle Maison to help Phil out with dinner. This little one has a summer cold, so I haven't been by this week, but I'm sure I'll stop in within the next few days."

"That would be great," Tamryn said. "Thank you so much."

"I'm more than happy to help," she said. "Anything that brings attention to Gauthier is a worthy cause in my book."

By the time the celebration wound down, the sun had already started to set. Tamryn was once again propped against the trunk of the oak tree where she'd observed most of the campaign kickoff event.

As Matt approached her, she couldn't contain the smile that broke out over her face.

"You ready to come claim that bag?" he asked.

"You're not going to make this difficult for me, are you?"

He shook his head. "I'm done being difficult. This will be very, very easy."

The mischievous gleam in his eyes should have sent her running in the opposite direction, but her good sense was having a hard time fighting the battle against the part of her that was aching to follow Matthew Gauthier and his sexy dimples to wherever he wanted to lead her.

As they exited Heritage Park, Matt made it a point to thank each of the workers they passed as they disassembled the tents, stage and other props used for the rally. There was a kindness about him, a sense of unpretentiousness that was endearing. Given his family's position in the community, he could easily flaunt his self-importance around, but Matt was as down-to-earth as any of the people she'd met here. In fact, he seemed to do his utmost to downplay his connection to the town's most powerful family.

They arrived at the Gauthier Law Firm and he held the door open for her.

Tamryn stopped just outside the threshold. "Why do I suddenly feel like an innocent little lamb being led by the big bad wolf?"

Matt's grin was as wicked as anything she'd ever seen.

"Do you want that bag or not?" he asked. "There's only one way to get it."

Her eyes narrowed with a wary look as she slipped past him and into the building. "I wonder what your loyal constituents would think if they knew you were holding my property hostage."

"No one would believe you. Not sweet little Matt Gauthier. He would never do such a thing."

Tamryn stared into his eyes. "You have them all fooled, don't you?"

Matt's fingers gripped her waist, and his forehead tilted down until it touched hers. "You have no idea." His whisper-soft voice held a hint of remorse. Before Tamryn could comment on it, he grinned and asked, "Now, are you willing to spring that bag free or not?"

"What's the ransom?"

"I think you already know," he murmured.

He dipped his head, his lips hovering just above hers. Tamryn knew she'd reached a critical moment. If she allowed his lips to touch hers, she was setting a course for how their relationship would play out for the rest of the summer. If she wanted things to remain on a professional plane with Matt, she should stop him right now.

Apparently, her sense of professionalism had deserted her in the two weeks since she'd arrived in Gauthier, because there was not a single ounce of her being that wanted to stop his lips from touching hers. In fact, of its own volition, her hand came up and cradled Matt's cheek as his lips descended upon hers.

His touch was light, his incredibly soft lips gently meshing with hers. He peppered her with feathery touches, just the tip of his tongue slipping out to tease her.

After a few moments, he became bolder, his kiss more ardent. He scooped his hand around, stroking the small of her back as he pulled her closer to him. Tamryn melted. Then and there, her insides liquefied into a warm puddle. She allowed him to pull her even closer as both his hands traveled up and down her spine.

His tongue traced along the seam of her lips before pushing inside. He stroked with subtle passion, a low groan crawling up from his throat.

Embolden by the sound she'd elicited from him, she sucked his tongue into her mouth, caressing it with her own. But then Matt took full command. He was both gentle and insistent, his tongue surging and retreating, exploring her mouth with bold strokes while his hands inched farther down her body, until they found a place to rest on her backside.

Matt tugged her closer, pulling her body flush against his and groaning with a pleasurable, painful sound.

Tamryn knew she had to put the brakes on this. Not only had she declared this a tingle-free trip — and her body was feeling nothing but tingles right now — but several of the people cleaning up Heritage Park had seen her enter the law office with Matt. If she didn't leave this office soon, Tamryn had no doubt that news of her and Matt's tryst would be the talk of the town.

"Matt," she said against his lips.

"Hmm?"

His deep moan sent delicious shivers down her spine. Delicious, *dangerous* shivers. She brought her hands up to his chest and gave him a gentle push. "Matthew."

"Don't ask me to stop," he murmured against her neck.

"Matt, please," she breathed. Maybe it was her *please* that caught his attention. He released her and took a step back, running a hand down his face.

Tamryn pulled in several deep breaths to clear her head. It felt as if she'd been deprived of oxygen.

After a few moments, Matt grabbed both of her hands and brought them to his lips. "Can you at least acknowledge what's happening here?" he asked.

"My skin is still tingling," she said. "It would be pretty hard to deny it."

His mouth curved in another of those half grins that only fueled those relentless shivers that continued to travel from the top of her head to the tips of her feet, stopping at all the interesting points in between.

"I wish I could deny it," she continued. "This wasn't a part of the game plan when I decided to come to Gauthier for the summer."

"Sometimes even the best-laid plans have to change, especially when something so good is waiting on the other side." Matt's forehead met hers again. "Whatever it is that's happening between us started the minute I pulled up to your broken-down car on the side of the road, Tamryn. It makes no damn sense to let all this chemistry go to waste." He kissed the tips of her fingers. "Let's just see where this leads."

"I'm only here for the summer."

"That means we have the summer."

"You just kicked off a campaign, and I'm in the middle of an intense research project."

"There's twenty-four hours in a day. I'm pretty sure we can both find a couple of hours we can spare. I promise you it will be worth it."

She pulled her bottom lip between her teeth, contemplating.

"Any other excuses you need me to shoot down with cold, hard logic?" Matt asked.

She shook her head.

"Does that mean I can kiss you again?"

She nodded.

Matt smiled.

And then he kissed her.

CHAPTER 6

Matt braced his hands against the granite countertop and lowered his forehead until it touched the cold stone. He longed to bang his head against it until he knocked himself unconscious, but then he'd just have to clean up the mess when he woke up.

He'd been on a conference call with Ben and several donors for the past forty-five minutes, and if it went on a minute longer he would have to find *some* way to put himself out of his misery.

As the men yammered, Matt walked over to the wet bar and, in a show of supreme strength, managed to bypass the scotch. As he poured himself a glass of mineral water, he let out a deep breath and tried to pull it together. These donors were eager to donate to his campaign, and for that alone they deserved his undivided attention.

Yet for most of the call his mind had been focused solely on Tamryn. She had been in town for just over two weeks, but Matt could barely go *two minutes* without having her face pop up in his head. For the past three nights he'd fallen asleep thinking about that kiss they'd shared after his campaign rally Friday night. He couldn't think of a single thing that was sweeter than her kiss, but it hadn't been enough to sustain him. He wanted so much more.

For days Matt had tried to pinpoint just what it was about her that turned him on so damn much, and last night he was sure he'd finally figured it out. Despite the fact that she had initially contacted him specifically because he was a Gauthier, when it came to the undeniable attraction simmering between them, she saw beyond the name.

He'd spent a lifetime dealing with women who were more interested in the clout they erroneously believed came with being a member of the Gauthier family than they were in getting to know him as a person. But Tamryn didn't look at him that way. She saw just Matthew. It was different. Refreshing.

The fact that she was sexy as hell didn't hurt, either.

"Matt? Matt!"

Ben's irate voice knocked him out of his musings.

"What?" Matt answered.

"You want to provide some input?" Ben asked. "What did you think of Donnelly and his partner?"

Matt had no idea the other men had left the conversation. He'd pretty much tuned them all out shortly after the conference call began, but it had been long enough for him to come to his own conclusions about Alfred Donnelly.

"I think he would be waiting outside the door to my office in the state-capitol building the morning I take the oath of office, ready to list his demands," Matt answered, walking over to the fridge and retrieving the cold pizza from last night. "I don't want donors who are looking for favors, Ben. I want people to support me because they believe in the work I want to do."

"You're in Louisiana. Don't think you can have a life in politics without doling out a few favors."

Matt squelched a sigh. How had he ended up with Ben as his campaign manager? Their philosophies were totally different.

He checked the time on the microwave and decided that he'd had enough of this for today. "Look, Ben, can we finish this a bit later? I have an appointment I'm late for," he lied.

"Yeah, yeah," Ben drawled. "Oh, I forgot to tell you that I talked to your dad yesterday."

Matt's spine went ramrod straight. "Why are you talking to him?"

"Because he knows what it takes to run a successful campaign," Ben answered.

Matt took the phone off speaker and put it up to his ear. "You can put that out of your head right now," Matt said. He started to pace between the kitchen island and the refrigerator. "There's no way in hell I'll allow any part of this campaign to be influenced by Leroy Gauthier. He has zero say in how my senate run operates, you hear me, Ben?"

"I don't get this, Matt. What in the hell do you have against your father? He's a respected appellate-court judge who won his seat by one of the biggest landslides in the history of the courts. Most candidates would kill to have an ace like that in his back pocket."

"I'm not most candidates. Leave him out of this." His tone brooked no argument.

"Fine." Ben's exaggerated sigh was like that of a twelve-year-old who'd been told to clean up his room. "If you don't want to take advice from someone who's been in your shoes before and came out victorious, that's your choice. I personally think it's the wrong choice —"

"I don't care what you think. Not when it comes to this."

"You're the candidate. But when you come to realize how much of a mistake this is, you take full ownership of it," Ben said. "Tomorrow we're doing prep for the first town-hall meeting. Remember that."

"It's on my calendar," Matt said. He ended the call with Ben, but continued to pace for several minutes in an attempt to calm down.

It wasn't working.

"Dammit," Matt whispered.

He'd told Ben from the very beginning that he didn't want his father anywhere around this campaign. Leroy Gauthier might have fooled the people in this town into thinking he was a stand-up, trustworthy pillar of the community, but Matthew knew him for the deceitful, cheating fraud that he was. His father was a Gauthier through and through, an amoral bastard who didn't care about anyone but himself.

He sure as hell had never cared about his wife or son.

Matt had made it his goal in life to never be like his father. The only thing the two of them had in common was practicing law, and Matt vowed to do everything he could to make sure that it remained the *only* thing they ever shared.

Once his father had moved out of the Gauthier mansion and Matt had moved in, he'd made it a point to erase as much of Leroy Gauthier from the home as he could. His first order of business had been relieving Marion Samuels of her duties as the Gauthier family's longtime housekeeper and cook. For years Matt had suspected that Marion's son, Leon, was his half brother.

Suspected?

Matt huffed out a laugh, shaking his head as he returned the pizza, uneaten, to the refrigerator. Leon looked more like his father than he did.

He wondered how many other bastard children Leroy had sired.

It took a moment for him to unclench his jaw. Matt ran a frustrated hand down his face, cursing Ben for bringing up his father and putting him in this mood. He wasn't up for dealing with this right now. He needed a distraction.

And he knew exactly where to find one.

This desire to see Tamryn bordered on ridiculous, but he couldn't help it. He *had* to see her.

Matt made his way to Belle Maison.

Maybe he could surprise her with a picnic lunch and a drive out to the Chalmette Battlefield. He would be bored to tears, but as a history professor she would eat up the chance to visit the War of 1812 site.

Matt's hastily concocted plan was annihilated when Phylicia met him on the porch at Belle Maison and told him that Tamryn was in New Orleans today, researching in the library at Xavier University. Matt shot a quick text message to Zeke Marsh, who hadn't batted an eye when Matt asked him to keep him abreast of the research Tamryn was conducting this summer.

Today, however, Matt didn't care about whatever it was she was seeking within the tomes of the university library. His only concern was making sure she was still there before he made the hour-long drive into New Orleans.

Did he really intend to drive all the way out there just on the off chance that he could convince her to have lunch with him?

"Hell, yes," Matt said as he slipped his sunglasses on and backed out of the driveway at Belle Maison.

He knew he had it bad. And he didn't give a damn.

■ ■ ■ ■

Tamryn ran a hand along the back of her neck, rubbing the kinks and knots that had taken up residence there. She'd been hunched over this table for the past three hours, unable to tear herself away long enough to even use the restroom. It had been this way for over a week. She was completely enthralled by every single article she'd come across.

She'd read about the history of the slave uprisings along the Mississippi River while researching her dissertation, but she'd never had the chance to delve as deeply as she'd always wanted to. She could spend months in this library and still not satisfy the curiosity that grew with every new text she pulled from the shelves.

"But if you don't get up from here soon, your bladder will burst," she mused.

She managed to leave her work long enough to use the restroom and grab a quick drink of water. When she returned to the archives room, Ezekiel Marsh was standing at the table she'd occupied since eight o'clock this morning.

"Hello there," he said as she made her way back to the table. "How's it going so far?"

"I could not be more jealous of you," Tamryn said.

He laughed. "I am very lucky to have this at my disposal."

"Beyond lucky. I was just thinking that I could spend a month in this room and not make a dent in this. The archives here at Xavier are absolutely remarkable. Thank you so much for allowing me such unrestricted access."

"My generosity is not entirely altruistic," he said. "I'm curious about your findings. Once you explained your research, I knew this was something I needed to hear more about. Are you making any progress?"

"I'm sure I would make a lot more if I wasn't sidetracked by every fascinating article I run across. And knowing that most of these places are just a short drive away is too tempting."

"You should definitely schedule a few day trips while you're here. There's living history up and down the river."

"I plan to take advantage of it whenever I can over these next few weeks. I cannot express enough just how much I appreciate this. I'll have to thank Matt for calling in a favor on my behalf."

"You can thank me with lunch."

Tamryn turned and spotted Matt coming

145

through the door.

"Speak of the devil," Ezekiel said, pulling Matt in for a one-armed hug. "I was just about to say that I need to get together with you, but unfortunately I've got office hours in ten minutes." He pointed to Tamryn. "Remember, if you need anything, just call or stop in at my office."

"Thank you," she said. She waited until Ezekiel exited the archives room before turning to Matt. She should *not* be so excited to see him, but she had a better chance of stopping a freight train with her bare hands than stopping the flutters flickering throughout her stomach. They had been there since the moment his lips had touched hers in his office on Friday night.

No, that was a lie. That tingly sensation had bombarded her the moment he'd pulled up to her disabled car, and it had only intensified with every encounter they'd had since her arrival in Gauthier.

She folded her arms over her chest and gave him a chastising frown. "Tell me you didn't come all this way just to take me to lunch."

"Only if you want me to lie," he said. He tugged her arms loose and captured her hands, pulling them around his waist as he buried his head against her neck.

146

Tamryn's eyes fell closed as her head tilted back.

"Matt," she said on a weak sigh. "Matt, you have to stop doing this."

"Not really," he murmured against her skin as his lips traveled along her jawline. "Three. No, four," he said. "That's how many times I had to stop myself from getting in my car and driving to Belle Maison last night, just so I could get another taste of you."

Tamryn told herself to put an end to this before things went too far. Anyone could walk into the archives room and discover them together. But her weak mental protests were no match for Matt's exquisite kisses. His hands gripped her hips, pulling her to him as his mouth continued its foray along her neck, his teeth nipping at her skin.

"Matt, please," Tamryn purred. She should have been asking him to stop, but instead it sounded like a plea for more.

Just as she was about to ask him to stop — for real this time — her stomach made an indelicate hungry growl.

Matt's deep chuckle resonated along her skin. "I guess that means you really want some lunch."

Tamryn's eyes slid shut again, this time in abject mortification. "I'm trying to think of the last time I was this embarrassed. I think it was back when I forgot all my lines during my third-grade Christmas play." She peered up at him, her face hot with humiliation. "I skipped breakfast this morning, and the granola bar I found buried in the bottom of my purse stopped being effective a long time ago."

"A granola bar?" Matt's brow narrowed with his censorious frown. "Now I see why your stomach is arguing with you. You're in a city that's known for its cuisine and you feed it a granola bar?"

"What can I do to persuade you to never bring up my noisy stomach again?"

His grin was pure sin. "You really want me to answer that?"

He didn't have to. The answer was more than obvious from his heated stare, and an answering heat flashed all over her body. Why did she have to meet this incredibly sexy man at a time when getting involved with him was the very last thing she needed? It was as if he was determined to keep her in a state of perpetual lust, and it was becoming downright impossible to fight it.

"I can tell by the way those cheeks are getting even redder that you don't need an answer. I love the way your skin blushes, by the way," he whispered against her lips. "It makes me want to come up with a bunch of other ways to make you blush."

"Oh, God, just stop," Tamryn said with a deep sigh. *Irresistible* didn't even come close to describing this man. She was in *so* much trouble.

"Come on." He laughed against her lips. "Let's get some food in you. And then I've got a surprise."

Tamryn looked up at him.

"Trust me. It's something your little history-loving heart will adore."

Two hours later, Tamryn found herself seated in the back of a horse-drawn carriage, the beautiful animal's heavy hoofs clopping along the narrow French Quarter streets. She tried to engage Matt in a discussion about the various historical structures, but his enthusiasm for history was pathetically lacking.

Once their tour was done, the carriage pulled up to the front gates that surrounded Jackson Square in the very center of the French Quarter.

"I think it's been long enough since lunch," Matt announced. He gestured with his head to the open seating area covered with a green-and-white awning. "No visit to the French Quarter is complete without a stop for beignets at Café du Monde."

"After the huge lunch we had at Antoine's? There's no way I can fit in more food. I think I've eaten more in the few weeks I've been here than I would have in two months back in Boston."

Matt took both of her hands in his and tugged her gently. She didn't resist nearly as hard as she should have.

He seated her at a wrought-iron table overlooking Decatur Street. A few minutes later, he joined her, placing a plate of the powdered-sugar-dusted French doughnuts, along with two cups of café au lait, on the table. Tamryn bit into the light dough and groaned. "Oh, my goodness, this is good," she said.

Subtle, sexy humor lit up Matt's eyes. "You're very vocal when you eat," he teased.

Her cheeks warming with embarrassment, Tamryn set the doughnut on the plate and dusted off her fingers.

"How very ungentlemanly of you to point that out," she said.

"It has to be the sexiest sound I've ever heard."

His gaze fell upon her lips, his eyes suffused with smoldering heat. Anticipation tightened her skin as Matt leaned forward. He reached across the table and swiped the corner of her mouth with the pad of his thumb. "Sugar," he murmured.

Tamryn released a shaky breath. "Thank you," she answered.

In that same low, seductive voice, he said, "Using my finger wasn't my first choice."

The current arcing between them was electric. The air? Magnetic. The sights and sounds of the noisy French Quarter faded away as they stared into each other's eyes.

Tamryn gazed at him, completely mesmerized. "You're dangerous, Matthew Gauthier."

"Maybe," he said. "But don't let that stop you."

She leaned forward, her lips inches from his.

And his phone rang.

Dammit.

Before he even knew who was on the other end of the line, Matt had already made the decision to murder him. He pulled the phone out and frowned at the number.

"I need to take this," he told Tamryn. He had to turn away because that dazed, sultry look on her face sent his concentration to hell. "Hello," Matt answered.

As he listened, his eyes slid shut. Corey Anderson, former major leaguer and current baseball coach of the Gauthier High

School Fighting Lions, described the scene at the home of his wife's grandmother, who was the head of the Gauthier Civic Association. This was just what he *didn't* need right now.

"Dammit," Matt cursed. "I'll be there in an hour. Try to keep the pitchforks out of their hands."

He ended the call and had to refrain from letting out another curse. Tamryn's face no longer held that sensual, kissable look. He wanted her face to hold that look all the time.

"Is there a problem?" she asked.

"You can say that." Matt rubbed the back of his neck. "Apparently, a member of the Gauthier Civic Association discovered that a group in Maplesville is planning to hold a carnival during the same week as Gauthier's African-American Heritage Festival." He brought his hands forward and massaged his temples. "There's been some . . . tension between the two towns ever since Maplesville got a new outlet mall."

Matt's stomach tensed every time he thought about that damn outlet mall. He cursed the day he'd ever contacted those developers. If it wasn't for him luring them to this area, that outlet mall wouldn't be here and he wouldn't have this secret weighing so heavily on him.

"Sounds like something the future state senator needs to get a handle on," Tamryn said. "I guess that means I'll have to get that tour of the Cabildo some other time."

"Sorry about that," Matt said. Then he grinned. "Actually, that's a lie. I'm not sorry at all. I remember going there on a field trip back in junior high school. I was bored out of my mind."

Tamryn's brows narrowed with exaggerated censure. "This lack of respect for all the wonderful history surrounding you is so disappointing."

"Maybe if I had a hot professor teaching me, I would have learned to appreciate it more." He walked around to her chair, but instead of pulling it back, he lowered his head and trailed his lips up the side of her neck. "I think a couple of lessons are in order. What do you think, Professor West?"

"I think if I had you as a student, I wouldn't get a bit of teaching done."

"That's the point," he said against her neck.

They returned to the university so she could pick up her car, only to discover that it had a flat tire. Matt's brows rose in surprised amusement as he listened to her light into the rental-car company's customer-service rep.

"Remind me not to get on your bad side," he said when she'd finished the call.

"I should have gone with another car-rental company after the busted radiator," she said, getting back into his car. "I'll call around tomorrow."

"Or you can borrow one from me," Matt offered. She twisted in her seat, her mouth agape as she stared at him in disbelief. Matt shrugged. "I have an old Toyota that's just sitting in the garage. It needs to be driven anyway."

"I cannot borrow a car from you," she said.

"You can if I insist," he said. "Consider it my apology for the hell I put you through dodging your calls and emails these past six months."

"Well, when you put it that way . . ."

Matt chuckled, shaking his head as he maneuvered onto the Pontchartrain Expressway and headed north. He steered the conversation toward Tamryn and her days of growing up in Charlotte, thinking that the less she talked about her research, the less chance there was of her bringing up something that he wasn't willing to share about *his* past.

It wasn't long before Matt realized that

getting her to talk about herself had less to do with keeping the spotlight off of him. The more she talked, the more he wanted to know about her.

"Do you get back home often?" he asked.

"At least once a year," she said. "My parents make the drive up the eastern seaboard every fall. They love the changing of the leaves. They come up to Boston, then take the drive with the other million tourists up through Vermont and Maine."

"I've always wanted to do that," Matt said. "The only seasons we have down here are hot and hotter."

"Tell me about it," she said with a laugh. "You should come to Boston. It's beautiful up there."

"Well, I know for a fact that there's at least one beautiful sight in Boston."

Her cheeks turned that adorable shade of pink again. It was so easy to make her blush. For what had to be the thousandth time, Matt cursed the fact that her lovely, inquisitive mind posed such a huge threat to his future. What he wouldn't give to have her be just a regular tourist visiting Gauthier because she wanted a taste of small-town life.

But she was here for a specific purpose — a purpose that could shatter everything he

155

held dear. He could not allow himself to lose sight of that.

Matt made the drive back to Gauthier in less than an hour. He pulled up to the white picket fence surrounding Eloise Dubois's yard. There were a least a half-dozen cars parked along the road leading to the wood-frame house. The setting sun sat just beyond the lush vegetable garden on the side lawn, turning the stalks of corn a brilliant orange.

Tamryn brought her clasped hands to her chest. "Oh, my goodness, I love the garden. I swear everything in this town just oozes charm."

As they walked up the porch steps, raised, agitated voices could be heard from within the house.

"Yeah," Matt said with a cynical snort. "I can feel the charm oozing out from every nook and cranny."

They entered the house and a hush fell over the den as a dozen wide-eyed stares traveled back and forth between him and Tamryn. The chatter went from quiet to a fever pitch as the older women bombarded them with questions while trying to stuff both him and Tamryn with homemade sweet-potato pie and finger sandwiches.

"We can get the skinny on what's going on between these two later," Margery Lambert said. "We're here to discuss this festival they're planning in Maplesville. Now, what are you going to do about this, Matt?"

The din of angry voices started up again.

Matt stood in front of the television and raised his hands. "Let's just calm down," he said. "What exactly is the problem?"

"From what I hear, it's the same group who convinced their chamber of commerce to allow the outlet mall to be built. They're planning some kind of customer-appreciation weekend. And they're trying to use the same carnival company that we were renting rides from for our festival. I want the Tilt-A-Whirl here in Gauthier."

That set off another round of heated arguments. Matt listened attentively to their grievances while he simultaneously tried to come up with a way to smooth this over so that constituents in both towns would be satisfied. The fact that he'd been so instrumental ushering in the thing that had driven such a huge wedge between the neighboring communities demanded that he come up with a solution. More and more, Matt wished he'd never heard of the Lakeline Group and their damn outlet mall.

"Ladies, please. Give me a minute to look into this. I'll call Councilman John Devereaux tomorrow. He just took over as president of the Maplesville City Council. We should be able to come to some sort of compromise. I won't stop until we do."

Eloise Dubois walked up to him and patted his cheek. "I knew we could count on you, Matty. Your mother would be so proud."

Her words caused the guilt eating away at him to mushroom, filling every bit of him with shame. Matt could only imagine the disappointment in his mother's eyes if she were alive to witness her son turning out to be just like the calculating manipulator she'd been married to.

Matt left the Dubois house with a promise to contact the civic association as soon as he had an update for them.

As they drove to Belle Maison, Tamryn regaled him with conversations she'd had with several of the women at Eloise Dubois's home. Her voice heavy with amusement, she maintained that he had Gauthier's entire female population wrapped around his little finger.

Matt listened with only half an ear as his mind toiled over the challenge he faced in trying to keep his part in bringing the outlet mall to Maplesville under wraps. He'd hoped that by now people's anger would have dissipated, but if the arguments he'd heard tonight were any indication, some in Gauthier were prepared to carry this resentment to their graves.

Not for the first time, Matt wondered what would happen if he just came clean about his role in this debacle. He quickly squashed that idea. Despite how popular he was with the people of Gauthier, Patrick Carter was a household name to the citizens in the other areas. If he was going to win this election, Matt needed every single vote he could muster from Gauthier's residents. If he lost any support at all with the people of his hometown, he could kiss that senate seat goodbye, and along with it, any chance he had of making it up to the people of Gauthier for all the strife he and his family had caused them.

That was the true catalyst for his desire to represent District Twelve. He couldn't turn back time and stop that outlet mall from being built, but as a state senator he could fight for Gauthier's residents. He owed it to them.

"Matt? Matt, what's wrong?" Tamryn called.

He glanced over at her. "What?"

"I asked you about your upcoming debate, but I think you've zoned out on me."

Without taking his eyes from the road,

Matt reached over, grabbed her hand and brought it to his lips. He placed a gentle kiss upon her soft fingers.

"I don't want to talk about the debate, or the campaign, or any of that other stuff. In fact, I don't want to talk at all. I'd rather just listen to you."

"You weren't listening to me," she pointed out.

"I was," he lied.

"Really?" She twisted slightly in her seat. "What did I say about the conversation I had with Mya Dubois-Anderson?"

"Um, that her baby is teething, or cooing, or whatever it is that babies do?"

"Wrong."

Matt shrugged. "I figured new mothers can't help but talk nonstop about their babies." He brought her fingers up to his lips again. "I apologize for not listening. I was trying to figure out what I can do to smooth things over between Gauthier's and Maplesville's residents. Believe it or not, the two towns actually got along at one time."

"Is there any way I can help?" she asked.

He glanced over at her. "You can tell me to keep driving past Belle Maison and come home with me."

Her sexy, throaty laugh rippled across his skin. "How is that supposed to help soothe

160

the tension between Gauthier and Maples-ville?"

"I don't know just yet, but give me a minute. I'm a politician now. I know I can come up with some kind of spin."

Tamryn leaned over and trailed a kiss along his jaw. "I'm not coming home with you tonight, but I have to admit that I'm tempted."

"Really?"

"Oh, yes," she breathed. Her voice was thick with what sounded like the same kind of desire that was rushing through his veins. "I haven't been so tempted in all my life, even though getting involved with you is the last thing I need right now."

Matt pulled up to Belle Maison, but left the car running. He unbuckled his seat belt and turned slightly toward her. "Come home with me," he said.

"I can't, Matt."

"Yes, you can." The words came out like a plea, but Matt didn't care. He needed the distraction she would provide the way he needed air.

He angled his body over the center console, shoving his fingers into her silky, wavy black hair.

"Come home with me," he whispered against her lips.

"Matthew, I can't," she said. Placing a chaste kiss on his mouth, she opened the car door and got out.

Matt shut his eyes briefly before exiting the car and walking over to the passenger side where Tamryn stood.

"Thank you for this afternoon," she said. "I had planned to tour the French Quarter, but it was much better having you as a tour guide."

"I think you have that twisted around," he said, capturing her by the waist and turning around. He spread his feet apart as he leaned back against the car, creating a space for her. "You were the one who played the role of tour guide."

"True, but I still enjoyed having you with me." She stepped up to him and gave him another of those quick kisses. They weren't nearly enough to satisfy him.

Matt pulled her closer and murmured against her lips, "It was my pleasure." He traced his tongue along the seam before thrusting it inside her mouth.

God, she tasted good. She tasted so damn good that, if he could, he would do this for the next twenty-four hours straight without ever once coming up for air.

A seductive whimper escaped her throat, stoking the fire that had exploded inside of him. Matt used one hand to cradle her head, holding her steady as his tongue dipped inside the warmth of her mouth. Over and over again his tongue plummeted, thrusting in and out, swirling around. Her sweet flavor drugged his senses, making it hard for him to think about anything but tasting more and more of her.

Dammit, but he wanted to taste more of her. He wanted his tongue on her body — *in* her body — licking and biting and sucking every delectable inch.

He grew hard; his fight to halt his arousal was no match for the desire building inside of him. His hips thrust forward of their own accord, matching the rhythm of his tongue.

She released another soft moan. The sound slid down his spine, caressing his skin, causing it to pebble. Matt dragged his hands down her sides and around to the small of her back. His palms dropped to her backside, and he pulled her closer, the need to feel her pressed up against him all but consuming him.

"God, Tamryn," he growled into her mouth.

Matt swallowed the shallow whimper that poured out of her.

"Matt. Matt, stop," she pleaded.

He could tell by the way she clung to him

that she didn't want him to stop, but she'd said the word, and that was all it took for him to put the brakes on. His mother had raised him to always heed a woman's request to stop, no matter what he thought she meant.

He released her lips, but not her body. His eyes closed, he dropped his forehead to hers and sucked in a deep, calming breath.

"I'm sorry," Tamryn whispered. "I just . . ."

"I know. You can't," Matt said. He ran a hand down his face.

"I won't be able to fight this much longer."

"But you're able to do so tonight," he stated.

She nodded. "I'm not even sure how, but yes, tonight, I'm able to put up a fight."

Matt blew out a breath and braced both of his elbows on top of the car's roof. He was as hard as a horny teenager on his first date.

"I'm sorry," she said again.

"Stop saying that." He trailed his fingers down her cheek and along her delicate jawline. "You don't have to apologize. I don't want you to do anything you're not ready to do."

"That's the problem," she choked out with a hoarse laugh. "I want to do it so badly that if I don't go inside right now we may just end up giving any guests who may be looking at us through their windows a free show."

"Don't tempt me," he said. "A scandalous sex tape just might be the thing to put my campaign on the map."

Her head flew back with her laugh. "I'm not sure that's the route you want to take."

"Ben would have a coronary," Matt said with a laugh. He leaned forward and whispered against her neck, "If I steal another kiss, will that get me in trouble with the teacher?"

"Why don't you try it and find out?" she suggested.

She closed her eyes and tilted her head back, but Matt only pressed a light peck on her forehead. She opened her eyes, looking up at him in confusion.

"If I did anything more than that I would have to follow you inside." He gestured toward the Victorian. "Good night, Professor."

"Good night," she said with a sigh. She lingered in his arms for a second longer before turning and heading for the B and B's porch steps. Matt maintained his stance against the car. His legs trembled with the need to follow her, but he managed to stay rooted to the spot until she entered the house.

Then he walked around to the driver's side, slid behind the wheel and grabbed on to it with both hands, holding on so tightly Matt was sure he'd find imprints of his fingers when he finally released it. It took all he had within him to finally turn the ignition over and pull away from Belle Maison, but he managed to do it.

Barely.

CHAPTER 7

Matt uncapped the bottle of water he'd grabbed from the refreshment table and looked over the large crowd gathered in the Gauthier High School auditorium. Matt hadn't expected his first public debate against Patrick Carter to garner many people, but interest in the campaign had escalated after the most recent commercial issued by Carter's camp.

His opponent's latest attack revolved around Matt's "string of women," as the ad stated. To say he was pissed off didn't even begin to describe the anger that flowed through Matt's blood just thinking about it. It was both inaccurate and out of line, and it cast him in the kind of light he definitely didn't want Tamryn to see him in.

Matt had showed her the video on his phone last night while they were at dinner — the third dinner they'd shared this week. He hadn't wanted her to see the commercial on her own and get the wrong idea. He'd explained that Carter had dug up every woman he'd dated since college.

He never professed to be a saint, but he wasn't some philandering playboy, either. He was single and had had his share of girlfriends, but he was fiercely monogamous, even when some of the women he'd dated had not been.

In the ad Carter had accused him of using his status as a Gauthier to "add to the notches on his belt" and that pissed Matt off more than anything else. He'd *never* used the Gauthier name as a means of getting women, even though some of the women he'd dated had pursued him solely because of his family's money and prestige.

Ben's response had been to hit back hard, and Matt had to admit that the desire to stoop to his opponent's level was stronger than ever, but he refused to sink that low. He would have to be satisfied with complete annihilation of his opponent in this debate.

Matt walked down the aisle of the auditorium, stopping along the way to chat with some of the people in the audience. He wasn't surprised by the number of Gauthier residents in attendance for tonight's town hall–style debate. Ever since the civic association had formed a couple of years ago, more and more residents had begun to take a more active role in things that concerned the town.

As he continued down the aisle, Barbara Cannon, wife of Lou Cannon, who owned the dry cleaner's on Main Street, stopped him.

"Thanks for contacting the parish government about the water pressure on Main," Barbara said. "They finally told us that they'll be here tomorrow to see what's happening with the line."

"Good," Matt said. "It took them long enough."

"At least you got them to contact us at all. I've been trying for a week."

"I'm just happy something is finally being done," he said. Something in Barbara's hand caught his eye. Matt stopped short. "What's this?" he asked.

"Oh, I found it at the house when I got home," she said, holding up the kind of flyer that hung on a door handle.

"Can I see this for a minute?" he asked.

He took the flyer Barbara offered. His blood began to boil with each word he read.

"Do you mind if I borrow this?" he asked.

"Not at all," she said. "Good luck tonight. You've already got my vote. Lou is the one who still thinks Patrick Carter is actually good for this place. I went cold on him a long time ago, ever since he voted to end the art program at the high school."

"That art program is starting up again next year," Matt told her. "We'll work on Lou."

He patted Barbara's arm and headed straight for the area behind the stage where he'd left Ben.

"What the hell is this?" Matt asked, holding up the flyer.

Ben folded his arms over his chest. "It's a list of all of Carter's past misdeeds, including the DUI everyone tends to forget about."

"He got that DUI before he got into office," Matt said. "It's not even relevant. And I told you I wasn't going this route, Ben. I'm not stooping to mudslinging."

"Do you want to win this thing?" Ben asked.

"Yes, but because I'm the right man for the job," Matt said. "Not because I'm the lesser of two evils."

"Whether or not you're the right man for the job is only about 50 percent of what will determine whether or not the people here will vote for you, Matt. You have to show them why they shouldn't vote for Carter." Ben held his hands up. "Look, you hired me to run this campaign because it's what I do. Trust me to win this damn election for you, Matt."

He slapped the flyer to Ben's palm. "I want these destroyed. I mean it."

Ben just rolled his eyes and shook his head.

"I mean it," Matt said.

"Mr. Gauthier, it's time." Matt turned toward the organizer of the town-hall debate, who was waving for him to follow her onto the stage.

He sat down on the stool on the left side of the stage and returned Patrick Carter's fake smile. Matt was so rattled after his blowup with Ben over the flyers that he stumbled through the first two questions, but when it came to the issue of defunding the elderly-assistance program, something Carter had tried to convince citizens would save money in the long run and put the burden of taking care of elderly parents where it belonged — on their children — Matt went for blood.

"Taking care of the elders of District Twelve isn't a burden, Mr. Carter, it's a privilege. When I was growing up, Mr. Boyd LeBlanc used to fix the bikes of every kid in Gauthier free of charge. Mr. LeBlanc no longer has family around to help take care of him. So who would bear that responsibility if not for our elderly assistance program?"

Matt turned to him. "Maybe if you had actually grown up in District Twelve, you would have a better understanding of just what it means when we say that we take care of our own."

"I've lived here for over twenty years," Carter blustered.

"It's not the same as growing up here. This area is in my blood. I know what it means to be a proud son of Gauthier."

Applause erupted from the crowd. Carter's face looked to be on the verge of exploding.

By the time the debate was over, Matt's earlier stumble seemed to have been forgotten. He stayed around for another forty-five minutes, shaking hands and assuring the people in the crowd that he would fight for them if he made it to the state senate. However, there were still a few who were not convinced that he was old enough.

"Carter has clout," Norm Donaldson told him. "He knows how to get things done in Baton Rouge."

"Patrick Carter didn't go into public office knowing how to get things done. He had to learn. I'm willing to learn, just as he did. I'm going to prove it to you, Norm. Give me a chance and I'll prove it to you."

The older gentleman didn't look convinced. Matt didn't know if he would *ever* convince some of them that he was the right man for the job, but he left the auditorium feeling more confident about his chances than he had when he'd walked in tonight.

He got in his car and drove right past the Gauthier mansion, heading straight for Belle Maison. After pulling into the lot, Matt quickly got out of the car and headed up the steps of the stately Victorian. He walked up to the front door and was about to knock when he heard, "How was it tonight?"

He whipped around and found Tamryn sitting on a white rocking chair on the huge porch.

"What are you doing out here?" Matt asked, walking over and planting a kiss on her lips.

"I was waiting for you. I haven't even gone inside. I figured you would be on your way."

"Am I that predictable?"

"I just figured that if you were anything like I am, you've been missing this," she said, pulling him in for another slow, hot kiss. Never leaving her lips, Matt pulled her out of the chair and switched places with her, settling her onto his lap and wrapping his arms around her.

"You're right," he said. "I've been thinking about that all day." He nuzzled her neck, planting delicate kisses along her throat. "What do I have to do to convince you to come home with me tonight?"

"Not nearly as much as you're probably thinking," she said. "I barely made it through last night's dinner without attacking you."

Matt slanted her a look. "Don't tease me," he said. He went for her neck again, giving the spot just above her collarbone a gentle bite. "If you're not ready for me to take you to my place just yet, I don't have a problem staying here with you."

"Do you know how many tongues would wag if people found out you spent the night here?"

"Baby, they are already wagging, believe me."

She laughed. "Seriously, how did it go tonight?"

He gave her a quick rundown of the debate, including the flyer Ben had made.

"I saw it on the table at breakfast this morning," she said. "They must have passed them out yesterday evening." She ran her fingers down his cheek. "It's admirable that you're refusing to go that route," she said.

174

"You don't need to. If anyone can win that seat based on his merits, it's you. You have been nothing but good for the people in this town, Matt. And they know it. I've witnessed that after only a few weeks here."

The people in this town had no idea just how detrimental he had been to it, but Matt didn't want to think about that right now.

"Why don't we go upstairs so you can tell me all about the exciting lecture you listened to tonight? Was it on Asia?"

"Egyptology," she said with a laugh. "And you know that if we go upstairs you will not let me get a word in about tonight's lecture."

"I'm not an ogre. I'd let you get at least three words in. 'It was good' should sum it up, right?"

"Actually, it was fascinating."

"See, three words. That's all I need to know about it. Now, let's go upstairs."

"How about I go upstairs, and you go home and rest after your successful debate?"

Matt dropped his head to his chest. The cold showers only worked to a certain point. He was going to spontaneously combust if he didn't release some of this pent-up lust soon, and the only release he wanted was the kind he would find in bed with Tamryn.

Because he was a damn Southern gentleman, he left her with a simple good-night kiss. As he drove home, his cell phone trilled. Matt glanced at the touch screen and frowned.

Great. Just who I don't want to talk to.

"Hello, Your Honor. What can I do for you?"

"Why didn't you hit Carter with his DUI tonight?" his father asked.

"I should have known you were behind those flyers," Matt said.

"I don't have time for playing around. I'm due in court early tomorrow morning, Matthew. I need to get to bed."

"Who's stopping you?" Matt asked. "You're the one who called me. Now, is there a reason you called?"

"Did you see that commercial Carter's camp threw together? You need to fight fire with fire, Matthew. I handed you the DUI. You should have used it."

"Forget it. I'm not bringing up old news just so I can sling mud at Patrick Carter."

"You get this softhearted shit from your mother. You need to grow out of it. You're not going to win this election playing Mr. Nice Guy."

Matt's grip tightened on the steering wheel.

"You need to get to bed so that you're up early for court tomorrow," Matt said.

"Goodbye." He hung up the phone before his father could say anything more to piss him off.

Too late. He was good and pissed, which was his typical state of being whenever he had an encounter of any kind with Leroy Gauthier.

Tamryn adjusted her earbuds as she jogged along the dirt path that ran parallel to the narrow two-lane highway. The only thing that stopped her from ignoring the alarm when it went off at 6:00 a.m. this morning was the promise of the homemade buttermilk biscuits that she knew would await her when she returned to Belle Maison. She was running for biscuits.

She turned onto the graveled driveway that led to a small recreation park, which boasted a baseball diamond and a running track. She spotted a black Mercedes parked under the twisty branches of a huge oak tree, and a smile drew across her face. She spotted the man leaning against the trunk of the tree and her smile widened.

Tamryn came up to his car and pulled out her earphones. She leaned over, putting her hands on her thighs and pulling in several deep breaths.

"Thank you," she said, accepting the

bottle of water Matt handed her. "And good morning."

"Good morning." His velvety-smooth voice was much too stimulating this early in the morning. "Are you ready to start my training session?" he asked.

"Training session?"

He nodded. "You offered to train me for this weekend's 5K, remember?"

Bracing one hand on the hood of his car, she bent her leg back and caught her right ankle, stretching her quad muscle. "Don't you think it's a bit too late to start training for a 5K you're planning to run this weekend?" Her eyes traveled from the top of his head to the tips of his running shoes, taking in the way his sweat-soaked shirt clung to his abs. "Besides, from where I stand, it doesn't look as if you need much training at all. I don't think I have anything I can offer."

Matt shoved off the base of the tree and sauntered toward her.

"I disagree," he whispered. "I think there's a lot you can teach me, Professor."

He shoved both hands into her hair, cradling the base of her head and holding her steady as his mouth descended upon her. Without releasing her, he moved them over to the tree and braced his hands on either side of her head. The knobby bark dug into her back, but her brain hardly registered it. All she could feel was Matt. She felt him on every single part of her body, from the tips of her feet to the very top of her head and all points in between.

One part in particular throbbed for him as his lips moved up and down her neck. He fitted himself more firmly against her, his hard length nudging her stomach. Tamryn closed her eyes and fell into the moment. She wanted him beneath her, inside of her. She wanted to tear the clothes off him right now and climb on top of him. She wanted to lose herself in him.

"Please, come home with me," Matt said against her neck. "This is crazy, Tamryn. I'm ready to lay you down and take you right in the middle of the damn park."

God, she wanted to go with him. Her body was *begging* for her to go with him.

So why in the hell wasn't she? Why was she fighting something they both so desperately needed?

"Okay," she said against his lips.

His head snapped up. "What?"

"Okay," Tamryn said, struggling for air. "Let's go."

Matt's eyes widened for a moment, then he snapped to attention, taking her by the hand and leading her to his car. Just as they reached it, a late-model brown sedan pulled up to them.

"Son of a bitch," Matt cursed under his breath.

The door opened and a portly man with a shock of white hair got out.

"Matt, I'm happy I ran into you."

"John. Hi," he said. He turned to her. "Three minutes. I swear, that's all it'll take."

Fifteen minutes later, Tamryn found herself jogging alone on the dirt path back to Belle Maison, her body humming with unsated lust. John Devereaux, the councilman from neighboring Maplesville, had not taken Matt's many hints, or just didn't care about the daggers both she and Matt threw his way as he rattled on about the upcoming fair in Maplesville that was scheduled for the same weekend as the festival in Gauthier.

Even the mouthwatering aroma of Phylicia's buttermilk biscuits wasn't enough to lift Tamryn's spirits as she entered the B and B. She'd finally decided to take that next step with Matt, and now that she'd been stymied, she was angry.

She slogged up the stairs to her room, grabbed the clothes she'd laid out before she'd left for her morning jog and went down the hallway to the bathroom. Most of the Victorian's other guests were still asleep, so she didn't have to worry about hogging the bathroom.

As she stepped under the warm shower spray, Tamryn closed her eyes and allowed her mind to drift back to Matt's heated kiss. The skill he possessed, the mastery he held over her body — it was hard to comprehend. After only a few kisses, he knew just where to lick and nip and suck. He knew exactly what to do to light her body on fire.

With his image front and center in her mind's eye, Tamryn let her hands travel down her stomach and into the thatch of curls between her legs. She slowly rubbed her fingers over the swollen flesh, massaging the pulsing bundle of nerves. She increased the speed and pressure, bracing her back against the tiled wall and adding her other hand to the action. In moments her body was erupting in a swift, all-consuming orgasm that caused her limbs to shake and her knees to buckle.

Tamryn sank to the narrow ledge at the rear of the shower and leaned her head back against the wall. By the time she was strong enough to step out of the shower, the entire bathroom was filled with thick steam.

She wiped at the mirror and stared at her

reflection.

"You have got to let that man have his way with you," she said.

Her body shivered at the thought.

As much as she'd fought this attraction to Matt, now that she'd decided sleeping with him was inevitable — even necessary — she wanted to do it now. Right damn now!

"That's what you get for playing hard to get," Tamryn muttered.

She got herself as dry as she could in the humid bathroom, but when she went to get dressed, she discovered her clothes had grown damp from all the shower steam. Tucking the towel securely around her, Tamryn opened the bathroom door and peeked around. Finding the space empty, she dashed down the hallway.

Her cell phone was ringing when she got back to her room. Tamryn smiled when she saw the name illuminated on the screen.

"Hey, you," she answered, tucking the towel more securely between her breasts as she sat on the bed and settled against the headboard. "I've been meaning to call you."

"I would hope so," her coworker Victoria said. "I can't believe you didn't call me already. You let me get this news like everyone else."

"What news?"

"What news? Didn't you see the announcement? I would have thought as a member of the History Department they would have told you before they told anyone else."

"I have no idea what you're talking about." Tamryn reached over and grabbed her iPad from the nightstand. She brought up her email and saw the subject line just as Victoria said, "Reid is the new head of the History Department."

The air whooshed out of Tamryn's lungs with the force of a two-by-four to the solar plexus.

"How? When?" Her eyes darted up and down the email, but her brain was too befuddled to take anything in.

"I got the email about an hour ago," Victoria said. "Did they seriously not tell the History Department beforehand? That's insane."

"They didn't tell *this* member of the History Department," Tamryn said.

Which more than likely meant that she would not be a part of the department for much longer.

Her heart slammed against her ribs as the full weight of that possibility struck her. It took some effort to swallow down the bile that had climbed up her throat.

"Vicky, uh, can I give you a call back a bit later?"

"Sure," she said. "I have to get to class anyway. It's a beautiful day here in Boston, so I'm not expecting many students to show up. Call me later. I want you to fill me in on the work you're doing."

"I will," Tamryn said.

As soon as she ended the call with Victoria, she dialed Brady Saunders's number. Brady was another untenured professor in the department. If he'd gotten news of Reid's new appointment the same way she did, she would feel at least a measure of relief. But Brady didn't answer his phone, probably because it wasn't even 8:00 a.m. yet on the East Coast.

Tamryn tossed the phone onto the bed and tried to calm her nerves. But telling herself to calm down was easy; actually doing it proved to be much more difficult.

She reminded herself that just because Reid was now the head of the department, it didn't mean that her position was automatically on the chopping block. If faculty members were dismissed, it would be done by committee. Reid would not have the final say.

But he wielded enough influence that Tamryn knew he could persuade others within the administration that she was dispensable, especially with the lack of publication credits under her belt. Publication credits she could have had if he'd included her name on the research she'd put an entire year of her life into. Instead, he'd taken all the glory.

Tamryn wrapped her arms around her stomach, brought her knees up and rested her forehead on them.

Everything she'd worked so hard for was in danger of being pulled right from under her. And without the diary that would prove her theory about her grandmother's past and help her complete her book, Tamryn couldn't think of a single thing she could offer that would save her job.

CHAPTER 8

The minute Matt ended the call with the school board's insurance company, which was now offering to settle Mrs. Black's case, he shot up from his chair and headed down the hallway.

"Hey, hey, hey. Get over here."

His footsteps halted at Carmen's summons. Matt walked over to her desk.

"I've got some checks you need to sign." She spread three checks out on her desk. Matt slipped a pen from the penholder and scribbled his signature on each. "You know, you can actually question what the checks are for every now and then," Carmen drawled.

"I don't worry about you stealing from me," Matt said over his shoulder. "I know where you live, and you and Scotty aren't leaving Gauthier anytime soon."

He walked over to the area of the law firm that had been cordoned off for months. Dr.

Lawrence and his crew of anthropology students were back, digging around and making notations in the marbled composition notebooks they all carried. An extra hunter had joined them today.

When Matt entered the room, the team was packing up their gear.

"Looks like I came in just at the right time," he said. "I didn't want to disturb you all."

"Feel free to come and go as you please," Dr. Lawrence said. "This is still your office, Mr. Gauthier."

"*Some* people wouldn't agree with you," Matt said. "According to *some* people, this area of the law firm now belongs to history."

"And I stand by that statement," Tamryn said, her brows hitched, just daring him to challenge her. That hint of sassiness was so damn sexy on her.

"Well, an argument can be made for that, too," Dr. Lawrence said with a chuckle. "We'll be back on Thursday. I have a colleague from DePaul coming into town. He'd like to see the site, if it's okay with you."

Matt nodded. "Be my guest."

The students and Dr. Lawrence started filing out of the room, but Tamryn stayed behind, lingering just outside of the yellow caution tape that the professor had replaced across the entryway. Matt leaned against the doorjamb and folded his arms across his chest.

"So, did you have fun today?" he asked.

The look she slanted toward him very clearly asked if he was out of his mind. "What do you think?"

"I think you had fun today," Matt mused.

"I spent the majority of the day completely enthralled." She held her arm up. "The goose bumps refuse to go away."

Matt pushed away from the doorjamb and sauntered toward her. In a purposely seductive voice, he said, "I can think of so many ways to give you goose bumps." A soft mewl escaped her lips as he nuzzled her neck. "I have a surprise for you," he said.

"What's that?"

"I'm stealing you away tonight for our first official *date* date."

"So all the times you've taken me to lunch and dinner over the past few weeks didn't count as official *date* dates?"

He shook his head. "Nah, that was just food. A real date is more of an event."

"What exactly is involved with you stealing me away?"

"Well, for one thing, it will require you to wear jeans — if you own any, that is."

"Of course I own a pair of jeans," she said

with a note of affront in her voice. "I'll meet you at the B and B. In jeans," she tacked on.

A half hour later, Matt stood in the grand foyer of Belle Maison, struggling to release a breath as he watched Tamryn walk down the staircase in a pair of hip-hugging dark blue jeans, a snug cherry-red sweater and high-heeled black boots. The only thing he could think about was scooping her into his arms and carting her right back up those stairs.

"Will this do?" she asked, plopping her hands on her hips and spinning in a slow circle. She gave her hips a little shake and he damn near lost his mind.

How was he going to get through the next three hours thinking about anything but peeling those skintight jeans down her thighs?

He nodded and sucked in a deep breath. "That will do just fine," Matt said after some effort.

"Am I setting one less spot at the dinner table tonight?" Phil asked, carting a tray of glasses. Matt reached to take the tray from her, but she twisted it out of his reach. "Thanks, but I've got it. So, you two are going out?"

"Yes, I'm stealing Professor West away for

the evening," Matt said.

A sly smile lifted a corner of Phylicia's mouth as one eyebrow pitched with curiosity. "Interesting," she mused.

Matt rolled his eyes, but laughed when he noticed the blush coloring Tamryn's cheeks. "I think you're embarrassing your guest, Phil."

"I'm just wondering how long it will be before news of this night out is the talk of Gauthier," Tamryn said.

Phil snorted a laugh. "There's been a betting pool going on at Claudette's since your first week in town. I'm happy I didn't get in on it. I would have been out a long time ago." She bumped Matt with her hip. "You're slipping. I would have thought you'd have convinced her to go out on a real date with you way before now."

"It wasn't for lack of trying," Matt said.

"Good for you for playing hard to get," Phil said, winking at Tamryn. "This one probably isn't used to that. You two have fun," she called as she continued on to the dining room.

"So, is that why you've been pushing so hard for a *date* date?" Tamryn asked when they were alone. "Because I've been a challenge?"

"What if I told you that was part of it?"

190

Matt asked, capturing her by the hips and pulling her closer. He trailed his nose along the soft curve of her jaw. "I figure the harder it is to win the prize, the sweeter it will be. You look stunning, by the way. Are you ready?"

"Thank you, and yes, I'm ready," she said. Her high-heeled boots made her nearly as tall as he, lining their bodies up with such perfection Matt almost found himself giving in to his earlier desire to take her straight upstairs.

Instead, he put a hand on the small of her back and guided her out the front door. When they stepped out onto the porch, Tamryn faltered.

"Why are you on that motorcycle?"

"You don't like my bike?"

"I like looking at *you* on the bike. As for myself? Not so much."

"You look damn hot on this bike. And in these boots?" Matt licked his lips. "Fantasy fuel."

"Fantasy fuel?"

"Hell, yes," he said, guiding her down the porch steps. "Something tells me that the way you look on this bike tonight is going to fuel my fantasies for the next month. At least."

Matt climbed on the Ducati and steadied

it between his legs. He turned slightly so he could watch Tamryn fit her foot on the back pedal and hoist herself onto the bike. The heat from her body against his back made him instantly hard.

Damn, this was going to be a long night.

Matt handed her the extra helmet he'd bought over the weekend. "Hold on tight. We're not going nice and slow this time."

"Matthew," Tamryn called over his shoulder in a warning voice.

He twisted around to face her, dropping his gaze to her lips before bringing it back to her eyes. "Trust me," Matt said. "Once you go hard and fast, you'll never want to do nice and slow again."

He felt the deep breath she drew. He had to take one of his own.

Matt secured her arms around his waist before revving the engine. When he took off down Belle Maison's driveway, Tamryn's high-pitched squeal carried on the wind.

They rode along the byways that hugged the mossy canals, passing far-spaced houses on stilts and fishing camps that dotted the edges of the swampland. The humid air was thick with the earthy aroma of the bayou.

They rode for a half hour before Matt slowed and turned onto a dirt road. He guided the bike down the winding, dusty path, underneath the arching, moss-laden branches of century-old oak trees. As they rounded a bend in the road, a huge wooden structure came into view. The scent of spicy food wafted over the graveled parking lot.

Matt parked the Ducati between two old-model pickup trucks, lowered the kickstand and removed his helmet.

"I should kill you for that, you know," Tamryn said as she took her helmet off.

"You know you loved it," Matt returned with a laugh.

"I think I left my heart somewhere on the road between here and Belle Maison."

"We'll pick it up on the way back," he said. He helped her off the bike, then took her by the hand. She wobbled a few times over the gravel, which only fueled Matt's love for those fantasy-worthy boots. With every wobble her grip on him tightened.

They approached a set of worn steps and Tamryn's movement slowed.

"Is this place up to code?" she asked.

"This building has been here at least a hundred years," Matt said. "If it's held up through all those hurricanes, it's not going anywhere. Trust me."

She eyed him with an unconvinced look and continued up the stairs. Matt was completely shameless in the way he outright stared at her shapely butt as she walked ahead of him. He was so tempted to snatch her back, drive his bike down to a secluded spot on the bayou and drape her across it. His tongue was aching to explore every inch of her smooth skin.

Not yet, he reminded himself. But soon. It had to be soon.

They entered Dooney's Crab House, which, on a Friday — one-dollar longneck night — was nearing fire-code limits. Despite the thick crowd, Matt and Tamryn had no trouble being seated within minutes of entering the establishment.

A few years ago, Dooney Boudreaux had put his business up as bond when his younger brother got caught up in a meth bust, then skipped bail. Dooney would have lost his livelihood if Matt hadn't loaned him the money to pay the bond. His brother had been found less than a week later, but at the time, no one knew that would happen. Dooney had told Matt that he would always have a place of honor in his bar, and the man had never gone back on his word.

They were seated and, within minutes, a platter of steaming crawfish was brought to the table, along with two icy beers.

"You are determined to make me eat these things, aren't you?" Tamryn said.

"Oh, yeah," he said. "No self-respecting Louisianan eats a crawfish the way you did at Doc Landry's picnic. Now, pay attention," Matt said, holding the shellfish up. He went through the proper motions of eating: breaking it in two, sucking the head and peeling the shell off the fleshy tail before popping it in his mouth. "Got it?" he asked Tamryn.

"I think so," she said. "But I'm not sucking the head."

"You have to suck the head," he said. "Sucking the head is the best part."

"You are so dirty."

A wicked grin spread across Matt's lips. "You're going to thank me for that later," he said with a wink.

It took her a few tries, but after about a half-dozen crawfish, Tamryn was tackling them like a pro.

"I can't believe I'm going to say this out loud, but I have to admit that I'm enjoying sucking the heads," she said.

Matt dropped the crawfish he'd been about to eat and closed his eyes. "Say that last part again, but slower, and with a little more of that sexy growl in your voice."

She slapped his arm, but when he opened his eyes he noticed her cheeks pinking. He couldn't wait to see that blush over every inch of her body.

She picked up her beer and took a healthy sip before setting the bottle back on the table. "If I want to stay awake I should probably switch to coffee," she said. "Today was exhausting."

"It looked as if you were enjoying yourself working with Dr. Lawrence," Matt commented.

"I was. The experience was amazing," she said. "Those goose bumps I showed you earlier had been on my arms all day. And you know what was even more enjoyable than watching history unfold before my very eyes? Watching those students as *they* watched history unfold. Seeing the way their eyes lit up, it reminded me of how my students would become so enraptured during the course of a class. I used to love that part of the job. You know, the actual teaching. I miss it."

"I don't get it. If you love teaching so much, why aren't you doing more of it?"

"You'd have to understand how academia works. And believe me, that's not something you want us to talk about on our first official *date* date," she said with a rueful grin. Then she shrugged. "I'll eventually get back into the classroom. But for now, I need to concentrate more on publishing. It's how you build your profile."

"And that's your goal? To build your profile?"

She tilted her head to the side, her gaze somewhere over his shoulder. "Honestly, I haven't thought about my long-term goal in a while. I've been concentrating so much on getting this book finished."

"And then what?" Matt asked. "Once the book is done, will you get back to teaching more than just a couple of classes a semester?"

"I haven't thought that far ahead yet. I keep hitting so many roadblocks. I'm not sure the research will ever be completed."

A tidal wave of guilt slammed into him, but Matt quickly squelched it. He refused to allow his sins to weigh down their night. Apparently, Tamryn had the same idea.

"You know what? No more talk about work or my research woes," she said. "Let's just drink beer, suck heads and have fun."

Matt tsked as he leaned back in his chair and took a long pull of his beer. "What would your students think if they saw you, Dr. West?"

She shook her head. "I'm not Dr. West tonight."

"I can go with that," Matt said. He brought his chair forward and said in a lowered voice, "Just remember that I have this naughty-professor fantasy. So, later on tonight, Dr. West might have to make an appearance."

The instant blush materialized and the only thing that stopped Matt from scooping her up and carrying her out of the building was Dooney Boudreaux picking that moment to walk up to their table. They chatted for a few minutes before Dooney's wife called for him from the swinging door behind the bar.

A man in an LSU Tigers T-shirt walked up to the microphone on the pieces of plywood that passed for a stage in the corner of the bar and put out a call for karaoke singers.

"You know, I've always wanted to do that," Tamryn said, gesturing to the stage.

"Sing karaoke?"

She nodded.

"Go on up there, then," Matt encouraged.

She shook her head. "I've got guts, but not that much."

"We're having fun tonight, remember?"

She regarded him with a challenging stare as the first singer walked onto the stage.

"Are you waiting for me to say it?" Matt asked. Her brow rose. "Okay," he said. "I dare you."

198

She set her beer down and lifted one of the premoistened towelettes from the basket on the table. She used it to wipe her hands, then pushed her chair back, stood and strode toward the stage.

Matt turned his chair around and straddled it, folding his arms over the back. Tamryn stood just to the right of the stage while the guy singing a song from a boy band from years ago wrapped up his number. She waited for him to leave the stage before stepping up to the microphone in those sexy-ass boots.

Matt placed two fingers in his mouth and let out a loud whistle. The crowd clapped as the emcee introduced her.

The first bars of a Mary J. Blige song began and Tamryn started singing.

Matt's jaw dropped. He stared at the stage in complete awe, unable to believe how god-awful she was. Not a single note was in tune. Her voice cracked as it went from low to high in the middle of the same note. It had to be one of the worst performances in the history of karaoke. All karaoke. Everywhere.

But to see her on that stage with her eyes closed and her body swaying from side to side made it all worth it. At least for him. The rest of the crowd looked to be in agony.

When she was done, Matt stood up and clapped loudly, whistling again and cheering her on. He didn't call for an encore for fear that they would be tossed out of the restaurant.

When Tamryn came back to the table, the smile on her face was a mile wide.

"I can't believe you did that," he said. "That was . . . uh . . . something."

"It was terrible," she said with a laugh "I know it was, but I don't care. That was *so* much fun." She put her hand to her chest; her eyes were bright with excitement. "I swear, I have wanted to sing karaoke for so long, but I couldn't do it in Boston where I know people. This was the perfect place for it. Now no one I work with has to know just how bad a singer I am."

"Unless someone captured it on a cellphone camera and you turn into a YouTube sensation," Matt pointed out.

She brought both hands to her cheeks as a look of horror stole over her face, but then she laughed. "You know what? I don't even care. It was worth it. It's been so long since I did anything like that. Just crazy, and silly, and free." She looked over at him, her eyes soft. "Thank you. I needed this tonight."

"You're welcome," Matt replied.

"Was I really that bad?" she asked.

"Yes." He laughed. "But if you wanted to do it again, I would walk down to that stage with you and cheer you on from the very front row."

"You would really do that for me?"

"Damn right. Even though the crowd would probably rise up in protest if they had to go through that again."

Her features relaxed into an easy smile. "Your brutal honesty stings, but I think you still might be the sweetest man I've ever had the pleasure of knowing."

She closed the distance between them and melded her lips to his. Matt soaked in her flavor, detecting her essence despite the spicy food and beer she'd consumed. Her mouth was sweet and delicate, and it tasted better than just about anything he'd ever had in his life.

He was completely lost when it came to this woman. Everything he thought he knew, everything he thought he held dear — his candidacy, keeping his family's lies hidden — all of it meant nothing when pitted against the chance to feast on Tamryn.

"Are you ready to get out of here?" he asked once they came up for air.

She opened her eyes; her lips hovered a millimeter away from his. "Where to next?" she asked.

"I haven't given you a proper tour of the Gauthier mansion yet," Matt said.

He studied her face as the smoldering look entered her eyes, and he knew that she understood exactly what he was suggesting.

"I think I'd like that," she said.

He released the breath he'd refused to take until he had her answer. Now that he had it, Matt knew that the half-hour bike ride back to Gauthier would be the longest of his life.

Neither saying a word, they gathered their things from the table. Matt dropped a fifty in the center of it, disregarding Dooney's insistence that his money was no good there.

He was ready to jump out of his skin as they made their way out of the bar. The anticipation of what was to come had him so on edge, he missed the kickstand when he first tried to release it. Matt took a moment to pull in a deep breath. Then another. He took several more, allowing his body the opportunity to find some control.

"Are we leaving?" Tamryn's warm breath fluttered against his ear, and all the control he'd fought so hard to find rushed out of him.

Matt turned and caught her lips in a deep, fierce kiss that left them both breathing hard. He handed her the helmet and said,

"Strap this on. We're about to break every speeding law in the state."

"I'm pretty sure that would be an unwise move for a state-senate candidate."

"I'm pretty sure I don't give a damn."

Matt revved the bike and took off, winding back the way they'd come. By the time he drove through the open fourteen-foot iron gate at the Gauthier mansion, he was holding on to his control by a flimsy thread. He drove down the driveway, parking at the back of the house.

Tamryn alighted from the bike. As he studied her legs in the skintight jeans, the bottom halves tucked into the equally tight, calf-high boots, the remaining bits of his hard-fought control vanished.

Matt climbed off the bike and took her by the hand. He fitted the key into the lock, but turned to her before opening the door.

"Just so we're clear, the tour comes after."

A sexy grin curled up the corners of Tamryn's lips. "You took the words out of my mouth."

Tamryn faintly registered the sleek stainless-steel appliances and ash-colored cabinetry as she entered the house through the kitchen door, but she scarcely had time for more than a passing glance.

The moment they got inside, Matt pinned her against the door and attacked her mouth, thrusting his tongue inside with a greediness that fueled her own passion. He gripped the hem of her sweater and pulled it up, his mouth leaving hers for only the briefest moment as he pulled the top over her head.

He gripped her backside, hoisting her up and wrapping her legs around his waist. She could feel his hardness through his jeans. It hit her exactly where she wanted him, needed him, *craved* him. She was awed by his strength as — her legs still wrapped around him — he carried her through the kitchen and up a large, winding staircase.

Tamryn tucked her head against his neck, inhaling his earthy, musky scent. She loved this side of him, the strong, cocky, self-assured biker she just knew was seconds from rocking her world.

They entered a bedroom that was just off the landing at the top of the stairs. Tamryn lifted her face from his neck and looked around. Her head reared back.

The room was completely white, with a canopied bed draped with delicate eyelet bedding, a painted rocking chair in the corner and a self-standing cheval mirror.

"This is your room?" Tamryn asked.

"Hell, no. But it has a bed. That's all we need."

He deposited her on the bed and hastily removed his T-shirt, leaving him in nothing but low-riding jeans. Tamryn's breath quickened at the sight of the evenly spaced ripples that cascaded along his stomach. On either side, just below his waist and above his hips, were sexy little indentions that just begged to be licked.

He reached down and captured her right foot, bringing it up to rest on his shoulder. His eyes closed, he ran his hands up and down her leather boot.

"I wish I could get those jeans off of you while leaving the boots on."

"You can't," she said.

He let out a sigh. "I know." He caught the zipper pull just below the back of her knee and tugged it down, slipping the boot off and dropping it to the floor. He repeated the process with her left leg. Once her boots and socks were gone, he grabbed her waist and pulled her closer, unsnapping her jeans and tugging them down her hips.

"Can I put the boots back on you?" he asked.

"It'll take too long. Hurry up and get undressed."

"You're right," he said, shucking his jeans

and underwear in one swift motion. "Dammit, give me a minute," he said before leaving the room.

Tamryn lay back on the bed and stared up at the lace canopy. Her entire body hummed, to the point that it felt as if she would burst clear out of her skin. Moments later, Matt returned carrying three condom packets linked together. He tore one off and ripped the packet open.

Tamryn scooted up the bed as he rolled on a condom. He climbed in next to her and dived for her neck, pulling the skin between his teeth as his strong, muscled chest met her soft breasts.

"This is going to go fast," he murmured against her skin. "Finesse will have to come later."

"I don't care about finesse," Tamryn breathed. "Just get inside me."

He swooped an arm under each of her knees and pushed her thighs up and back, entering her in one steady, sure thrust. Tamryn's head fell back as every pleasurable feeling she'd ever experienced before seemed to converge. She melted into a hazy puddle of sensation as Matt drove his hard length into her. He knew exactly where to stroke, exactly how much pressure to apply. He knew when to hold back and when to go deeper. It was as if they had been making love to each other for years instead of only minutes.

Tamryn closed her eyes and concentrated on the feel of him. His hot, silky flesh felt like heaven as it penetrated her. It was intoxicating. The pleasure he delivered was something she knew her body would come to crave. She already craved it. With every deep, seductive slide of his steely flesh, her body wanted more. He shoved his hands underneath her, clutching her bottom and holding it steady as his hips surged and retreated.

Sensation began to build low in her belly, slowly fanning outward to all her extremities, until her limbs started to tremble with it. Matt's open mouth clamped down on her shoulder and her entire being erupted as wave upon wave of pleasure soared through her bloodstream.

Tamryn cried out, her screams echoing off the walls. As her body shivered, Matt continued to pump his hips with fevered abandon, thrusting in and out until, finally, his body stiffened and he growled his release.

He collapsed on top of her, his lips falling on that spot behind her ear.

Tamryn lay supine on the bed, staring up

at the lacy canopy that stretched from the four ornately carved bedposts. It took effort just to pull air into her lungs.

"I don't know why I fought this for so long," she said.

Matt's deep chuckle reverberated along her skin. He moved onto his side and pulled her naked body flush against his. He drew a lazy finger down her arm and along her side, over her hip and down to her thigh. He sucked on her bare shoulder, trailing his tongue over her moist skin.

"You are so sexy," he murmured as his lips drifted to the curve of her throat. He peered at her. "I need you in those boots. Oh, wait, no. The reading glasses. I need to live out my sexy-history-professor fantasy."

She laughed. "You are so warped."

"I'm dead serious."

She twisted around in the bed and wrapped her arms around his neck. "I'll make sure to bring them next time," she said, placing a quick kiss on his lips.

"I like that you're already thinking of next time," he said.

"Well, I still have two weeks left in Gauthier. I figure we can do this as often as possible. Now that I know what I've been missing, I'm sorry I held out for so long."

Matt sobered. "Are you really down to just

two weeks?"

She pulled her bottom lip between her teeth and nodded. "I know. It's gone much quicker than I thought it would."

"When do classes start up again?"

"The last week of August, but the faculty has to be there the week before."

"That's nearly six weeks away. You could stay in Gauthier for another month and still have time to get things ready for your next semester."

Just the thought of extending her stay sent a flutter of pure elation through her stomach, but Tamryn swiftly suppressed it.

She shook her head. "I can't stay here another month. Never mind the fact that I would go broke if I had to pay for four more weeks at Belle Maison —"

"Stay here," he interrupted her.

"What?"

"Stay here. We could get your things tomorrow. Phil and Jamal have a waiting list of people wanting to stay at Belle Maison, and if they can't rent out your room, I'll pay for the remaining two weeks you have there."

"Matthew," she said.

"What? It's not as if everybody in town hasn't been betting on when we're going to get together anyway. Why not stay here with me?"

"Matt, I can't."

"Tell me why not," he persisted. "Give me one good reason why you can't stay here. And it has to be a *good* reason."

"So, 'because' won't work?" she asked with a grin.

"No. 'Because' is not a good enough reason."

She shrugged her bare shoulders. "I can't think of one right now. I just . . . I don't know. You're the one who's in the middle of a political campaign," she pointed out, poking his solid pectoral muscle. "You're the one who should be concerned about rumors."

"I'm a grown man. Who I have staying in my house with me has nothing to do with my ability to serve the good citizens of Gauthier." He took her hand and pressed a kiss to the back of her fingers. "And if that's the best excuse you can come up with, I say we head to Belle Maison right now and get your things."

"I can't," she said with a laugh. "Not because I don't want to, but because I have too much work to do. And after what we just did, you're now at least ten times the distraction you were before tonight."

"I like being a distraction," he whispered as he dipped his head down and captured her lips in a slow, sweet kiss.

Tamryn closed her eyes and soaked in the intoxicating feeling of his mouth against hers, loving the patient care he employed as his tongue gently plunged in and out. It would be so easy to take him up on his offer. To spend the next two weeks — the next *six* weeks — nestled against him in this massive, historic home. *Heaven on Earth* couldn't begin to describe it.

But she couldn't. Not when she was as far as ever from meeting the goal she'd set out to accomplish when she'd arrived in Gauthier. With a reluctance like none she'd ever experienced before, Tamryn managed to pull away from his drugging kiss.

"God, you're good at that," she said. "And that's the main reason why I will be returning to Belle Maison. I would never get any work done if I stayed here with you."

Matt let out a groan. "Work, work, work. You're worse than an attorney," he said with a playful wink.

Tamryn burst out laughing. She placed a swift kiss on his mouth before twisting around and, once again, settled her back against his chest.

"Remind me again why you're making this

big push to get your research done by the end of the summer? Didn't you say that you've been researching your grandmother's past for years?"

"Yes. And that's part of the problem. I've been researching it for far too long. It's time I stop lollygagging and get it done."

"The fact that you just used the word *lollygagging* in a sentence makes me much happier than it probably should."

Tamryn rolled her eyes.

"But there has to be more to it than you just crossing off an item on your to-do list, right?" Matt continued. "You want the career boost that you're hoping the book will give you."

"And now I need it more than ever," Tamryn said.

She felt him stiffen. "Go on."

"You don't want to hear about this tonight, Matt."

"Go on," he encouraged.

"Fine." Tamryn sighed. "Remember when I mentioned that there were some issues at work?" She felt him nod against the crown of her head. "Well, that issue happens to be the new head of the History Department."

"Sounds as if the history there is more than what you find in books."

"Unfortunately, yes. He had been in the

212

department for about five years when I first started at Brimley. He took me under his wing, helped me to work through all the bureaucratic stuff."

"And?" Matt prompted.

"And I fell in love with him."

"But you're not anymore?"

"Oh, no," she said. "I am so far out of love with him that I can't remember what loving him feels like."

"The two of you had a falling-out?"

She huffed out a humorless laugh. "You can say that. This past fall, he was awarded a grant for a project that we worked on together. I put my research on the side for over a year so that I could concentrate on his research project. He's been showered with accolades from all corners of academia." She paused. "My name isn't anywhere on it. We were supposed to be coauthors of the paper, but he took my name off before submitting the documentation."

"Son of a bitch," Matt cursed. "Who does something like that?"

"Dr. Reid Hayes," she answered. "When I confronted him about it, he told me that I should be grateful that he allowed me to work on the project at all. He also said that if it wasn't for the fact that I was screwing him, I would be working at some junior college."

"That's bullshit," Matt said. "I can tell you're ten times better than half the professors who taught me just by observing your work ethic. Your dedication to your research continues to amaze me, Tamryn."

"I know I'm damn good at my job, but I won't deny that Reid's words put a chink in my confidence. He *did* help me to get my position at Brimley. It was before we started sleeping together, but did he recommend me just because he wanted to sleep with me? How will I ever know?"

"Don't." Matt captured her chin and tilted her face up to his. "Don't allow him to do that to you."

"You're right," she whispered. She took his hand and brought it around her torso so that his forearm rested just below her breasts. Staring at the swath of moonlight that cut through the lace curtains, Tamryn said, "But I still want to prove to him that he did not make my career. Having this book published by a distinguished university press will mean a lot for me on a professional level, but the chance to rub it in Reid's face — to prove that I can stand on my own merits in the academic world? That's what really drives me.

"I just need to uncover that one piece of evidence that will bring all the research together. I know it's there, Matt. I can feel myself getting closer. Everything points to my grandmother and Nicolette working together to start that school for slave children. I just need to find the proof."

"You will," he whispered against her temple.

Tamryn pulled his arms more firmly around her, relishing in the strength emanating from him. Those two words gave her hope that she would eventually uncover what she'd come to Gauthier to find.

As she rubbed her hand up and down his arm, a part of her realized she'd already found more than she'd ever expected.

CHAPTER 9

"Hey." Matt pulled up next to Tamryn as she bent over and rested her hands on her knees. "I thought you were a runner?" he said, tugging on her ponytail.

She straightened and shot an evil look his way. "I usually run four miles a day. I'm just not used to running after having so little sleep the night before."

Matt didn't even try to stem the wicked smile that drew across his face. "Don't think you're going to get me to apologize for that, because it's not gonna happen."

"I wasn't expecting you to apologize. In fact," she said, closing the distance between them, "I won't be all that upset if you make tomorrow's run even more difficult."

Matt waited for the shiver to rush through him before he attempted to speak again. "You're trying to get me to embarrass myself in front of all these people, aren't you?"

"And just how would I do that?"

"Wait a minute and look south. You'll know exactly what I'm talking about."

Her eyes darted to the front of his rayon basketball shorts, which were loose but not nearly baggy enough to hide the hard-on that was minutes from making its presence known if he didn't get a handle on his overcharged libido.

Being in such close proximity to Tamryn wasn't helping, but walking away from her was beyond his current capabilities. He wanted to grab her and kiss the smile right off of her face. Dropping her off at Belle Maison this morning had been harder than he could have ever imagined.

Matt had spent the majority of the ensuing hours unable to think about anything but her lips, and hips, and those delectable thighs. He could feel them wrapping around his waist. If he closed his eyes, he could see the tiny ankh symbol that had surprised the hell out of him when he'd discovered it high on her hip. The professor was full of little surprises, and he was having more fun than he ever thought possible uncovering them.

Only one thought dampened his mood — knowing that he had the diary she was still desperately searching for. For the briefest moment last night he'd considered taking it out of the safe in his family library, but Matt had quickly disregarded the idea. He had too much to lose if the secrets within those pages ever came to light.

Instead, he'd remained in bed snuggled against Tamryn's soft warmth. He knew he was being selfish, but he wanted to put all of the lies of omission out of his mind and just enjoy his time with her.

After dropping her off at Belle Maison this morning, he'd come straight here to help Carmen and the volunteers she'd secured get ready for the race. They'd set up several water stations along the 3.1-mile course that wound through downtown Gauthier and several of the residential streets before ending at the waterwheel in Heritage Park.

He and Tamryn headed for the base of Main Street, where volunteers were instructing participants on how to line up for the 5K.

"Remember, runners in the front, walkers in the back," Isaiah Ryder, the track coach at Gauthier High School, called to the crowd.

"Are you running or walking?" Tamryn asked, widening her stance and stretching her arm over to one side.

"I usually run it, but after last night, I don't know," Matt said. "I think my body needs a little recuperation time."

"Shh," she hissed, her eyes darting from side to side. "You're too loud."

"Do you realize how cute you are when you're blushing?" he said, swooping in for a kiss.

Tamryn swatted him away before his lips could make contact, and pointed just over his shoulder. Matt twisted around and discovered that they were the main event. About a dozen eyes were watching unabashedly. Several of the ladies, most of them members of the Gauthier Civic Association, gave them the thumbs-up sign, and they all had broad smiles on their faces.

"Oh, great." Matt snorted. "By the afternoon we'll be engaged and you'll be picking out wedding china."

Her eyes sparkled with laughter. "I just love this small town."

Matt snorted again.

Several minutes later, the group of nearly two hundred runners, which was mostly made up of kids from the middle and high schools, were lined up and ready to go. Coach Ryder shot blanks into the air, signaling the start of the race.

Matt set out on an easy jog in the center of the pack. After the first mile, he told Tamryn that he wanted to go to the back to see how the older residents who were walking the route were doing. She jogged alongside him, keeping pace. A sexy sheen coated her body, making him itch with the need to run his hands all over her.

Matt sucked in a deep breath, willing his body to calm down. If he had a snowball's chance in hell of getting through today without showing all of Gauthier just what was on his mind right now, he would have to pull himself together.

Tamryn joined him in manning the race, jogging back and forth several times, until Eloise Dubois, accompanied by her daughter, Maureen, granddaughter, Mya, and great-granddaughter, Kamri, made it to the waterwheel in Heritage Park an hour and a half after the start of the run.

Over the years, the celebration after the 5K had grown into an event in its own right. There were games for the kids, along with myriad snacks for runners and spectators.

Matt was handing out bottles of Gatorade donated by Cannon's Dry Cleaner's when Corey Anderson, the pride of the Gauthier Fighting Lions baseball team who'd had a short career in the major leagues before returning to coach at the high school, walked up to him. His baby girl was fast asleep in his arms.

"How's it going, Matt?" Corey asked.

"Pretty good, don't you think?" Matt answered. "The turnout was even better than I anticipated."

"If there's one thing you can count on from the people of Gauthier, it's supporting the cause," Corey said. "It's what makes living here so special."

"I hear you. Thanks for getting your baseball players involved."

"It was either run the 5K or run twice that much during practice." Corey laughed, but then he sobered and his voice took on a hesitant edge. "Hey, Matt, want to step over here?" He tipped his head toward a wooden bench.

Matt's brows drew together. He handed a couple bottles of Gatorade to the kids waiting in line, then dried his hands on the hem of his T-shirt as he followed Corey a few yards over to the bench.

"What's up?" Matt asked, taking the seat next to him.

"I've been meaning to talk to you about this for a while, but as time went on without you ever bringing it up, I figured it was something you just weren't planning to share."

"What are you getting at, Corey?"

"You know that I was originally a big

proponent of that chain retail store that was proposed for Main Street last year, right?"

A thread of unease traveled down Matt's spine. That retail store had opened up many of the old wounds first created by the construction of the Maplesville outlet mall. The residents of Gauthier were convinced it would destroy many of the businesses on Main Street.

"What about it?" Matt asked.

"The same developers who were seeking to bring the retail store were the ones who built the outlet mall over in Maplesville. They mentioned some of the other supporters."

"Look, Corey —" Matt started, but the other man stopped him.

"I'm not saying anything one way or the other, Matt. I know that a lot of the people around here were against the outlet mall and it's caused a lot of negative feelings between the two towns."

"Corey, I didn't know the developers were going to go to Maplesville," Matt said. He put his elbows on his thighs and ran his palms down his face. "This has all turned into the biggest damn mess."

"Look, Matt. If it *does* come out, I don't think you have anything to worry about. The people here are pretty forgiving."

"I don't know about this one," Matt said. "The controversy surrounding this outlet mall is bigger than anything this town has ever seen. If people find out that I was the one who first sought out the developer, they'll accuse me of trying to bankrupt the town."

"Were you?"

"Hell, no, Corey! Come on! That's the exact opposite of what I was trying to do."

"I'm sorry I even asked that. I know you would never intentionally do anything to hurt Gauthier, not with all your family has done for this town."

It took everything Matt had within him to hold in his sardonic snort.

Yeah, his family had done a lot for this town. He could count on one hand how much of it was good.

The baby in Corey's arms began to squirm and, seconds later, started to wail louder than a police siren. Matt stared at Corey's retreating back as he made a beeline for his wife. He couldn't help but wonder if what the other man said was true. Would the people of Gauthier forgive him if he just came clean and explained his intentions when he originally sought out the Lakeline Group?

Later that night, Matt lay in his bed with

Tamryn nestled against his chest. He stroked up and down her arm, relishing the feel of her dewy skin.

"Why are you so quiet tonight?" she murmured.

"Because you wore me out?" he replied, pressing a kiss to her temple. "I'm pretty much speechless."

"You are such a politician," she said. "You always come up with the perfect response."

Matt felt her body vibrate with laughter, but he didn't join in.

Tamryn peered up at him over her bare shoulder. Her forehead furrowed as she studied him.

"Matt, what's going on?" she asked, twisting around so that she faced him. "You've been . . . I don't know . . . off most of the afternoon." His brows arched as his eyes drifted languidly down her body. "Well, except for what you just did a few minutes ago," she added.

Even her adorable blush couldn't wring him out of his sour mood.

Matt hauled her on top of him and settled his hands on her lush backside. She lay on her stomach, her breasts crushed against his chest. He could easily spend the next week in this position. Tamryn's apprehensive expression stated that she clearly could not.

She wanted answers.

He pulled in a deep breath and debated the wisdom of sharing this. There was so much he was keeping from her already; it would be cathartic to finally let some of it out.

"I have a confession to make," he started.

Matt felt her entire body stiffen. Her uneasy gaze roamed over his face. "You're not married, are you?"

He speared her with a sardonic look. "Don't you think the people in this town would be lining up at Belle Maison to tell you if I was married?"

"Good point." She pressed a kiss to his left pectoral, then folded her hands on his chest and rested her chin on them. "So, what's the deep, dark secret you want to share?"

Matt stared up at her and, for the briefest moment, had an overwhelming urge come clean about it all. He thought of the wall safe downstairs, hidden behind a framed portrait of his ancestor. He thought about the leather-bound diary that resided inside of it and how it contained the very thing that had brought her into his life, the very thing that could possibly save her job: the story of *her* ancestor.

But it was also filled with his aunt Nicolette's detailed accounts of many of the wrongdoings early members of the Gauthier family had engaged in. Once the floodgates were opened, it would take very little digging for someone to unearth some of the other transgressions the Gauthier men had committed throughout the years. Some illegal, some just unethical, but all were offenses that would mar his family's name in this town forever.

The people of Gauthier loved the town's founding family. Preventing those stories from coming to light wasn't just for the sake of saving his campaign or his family's reputation; it was for the sake of all the people living here who needed to believe that the Gauthiers were everything that was good about this small town.

The load of bull he'd just fed himself was hard for Matt to swallow, but it did just enough to stop him from spilling his guts to Tamryn.

Instead, Matt said, "I explained to you about the outlet mall in Maplesville and the rift it's caused between the two communities, right?"

"You and several other people around here," she said.

He hesitated, then admitted, "I'm the one who brought this area to the developers' attention."

Tamryn's head popped up. "What do you mean?"

"A couple of years ago I ran across an article about this development group who had built outlet malls throughout the southeast. They were looking for another site. There were people on both the pro and con side, but the pros seemed to have the better argument. Tax revenues, jobs, lots of prosperity — all the things I wanted for Gauthier."

"So how did the outlet mall end up in Maplesville?"

"The developers got a better deal on the land, and there was more of it. They were able to buy huge acreage and, in the couple of years since they moved in, have sold it to other developers. Now there are retail shops and strip malls popping up all around Maplesville, and the shops in Gauthier are feeling the pinch."

"The pinch? None of the businesses on Main Street seem to be struggling to me."

"Well, they're not now. Not with the tourists that have been brought to town because of last year's revitalization efforts and the Underground Railroad discovery."

"So what's your point, Matt?"

He looked at her as if she were crazy. "The

point is, I could have single-handedly ruined this town."

"But you didn't. In fact, according to Mya Dubois-Anderson, if not for that outlet mall, the Gauthier Civic Association would have never gotten the revitalization effort off the ground. She said their anger over the outlet mall was the catalyst for all of that."

"True," Matt agreed.

"She also pointed out that, if not for a fact-finding mission she and Corey went on because of the revitalization effort, that discovery at the Gauthier Law Firm probably never would have happened."

"But Mya can't be sure about that. It's possible it would have been uncovered in some other way."

"That secret room had been under everyone's noses for a century and a half without being uncovered. In the end, the outlet mall was a blessing, Matt. Don't think about what it could have been — think about how it's all worked out for the good of Gauthier."

"Yeah, but —"

"But nothing." She looked at him with such compassion in her eyes. "Please tell me you haven't been stressing yourself out over something like this."

"You don't understand."

"Yes, I do," she said.

No, she didn't. She didn't realize that this was just one notch on a long list of awful things his family had done to this town. She didn't realize that he was willfully hiding the very information that she was seeking to uncover. There was *so* much she didn't understand.

"Matt, the people in this community absolutely adore you. I swear, it's downright nauseating to witness how much they dote on you. Do you really think they would fault you for something like this?"

"Maybe you're right," he said.

"I know I am. I'm the professor here, remember? The professor is always right," she quipped. She stretched up a few inches and pecked him on the lips. "No more worrying about this, okay?"

Matt nodded. He couldn't tear his eyes away from her understanding, sympathetic gaze. The longer he stared into those warm brown eyes, the more he hated himself for the lies that continued to exist between them.

His throat tightened with emotion as he tried to weigh the impossible decision that lay before him. If the information buried within the pages of that diary ever surfaced, not only would it destroy the Gauthier name in this town, but Patrick Carter would use it to eviscerate him. He could kiss his hopes of representing District Twelve goodbye, and with it, all chance of righting some of the wrongs his family had done to this town.

How could he choose between the woman he was quickly falling in love with and the town he owed so much to?

CHAPTER 10

Tamryn stood off to the side of the lecture hall, just to the right of two huge double-paned windows of the stately administration building on Xavier University's historic campus. She could not suppress her excitement as she took in the rapt expressions on the students' faces. Their eyes were bright with interest as Ezekiel Marsh gave an overview of the research Tamryn was doing here in Louisiana.

"Dr. West has agreed to take time out of her busy research schedule to talk with you all today, so don't embarrass me by asking asinine questions," Ezekiel said with a grin. He gestured for her, and Tamryn started for the front of the classroom.

She assumed a relaxed pose against the podium and expanded on Ezekiel's description of her overall research, getting much more in-depth when she started to speak about what led her to Louisiana. The air around the room hummed with a sense of anticipation as she discussed the clues she'd uncovered about Adeline West and other women of color whose impact on the history of African-Americans had been ignored. Tamryn was motivated by the engrossed looks on the students' faces, their captivated expressions spurring her on.

As she fielded their inquiries and joined in on their discussions, she felt a sense of purpose that she had not experienced in a long time.

This was what had been missing.

This was what she loved; it was why she'd gone into teaching.

Seeing the enthusiasm on the students' faces, witnessing their eyes light up as they learned of the abundance of rich history right here in their midst — that was what made her job special. Gaining renown within her field had always been a goal, but Tamryn realized that she'd allowed it to become everything to her. Just as she'd allowed this overwhelming desire to prove herself to Reid to consume her this past year.

None of that mattered. The only thing that *truly* mattered was shaping the minds of young students who had that same zeal for history that had been instilled in her by her grandfather. And finally uncovering the truth about her great-great-great-grandmother — not for the esteem it would bring her when she published her book, but because she owed it to Adeline West. This project was not about her career; it was about a young, brave freed slave getting the recognition she deserved for her courageous actions nearly two centuries ago.

Once the class ended, Tamryn followed Ezekiel back to the suite of offices that housed the History Department. He offered her a cup of coffee and carried both cups to his office, handing hers to her as she sat in the chair in front of his desk. Instead of going around his desk to his comfortable leather desk chair, Ezekiel sat on the hard wooden seat that faced her.

"Thanks for doing this," he said. "I think the students enjoyed hearing someone other than me for a change."

"Are you kidding? I'm the one who should be thanking *you.* I enjoyed every minute of that." She took a sip of her coffee, cradling the foam cup in her hand. "You know, it's been a while since I taught students so young. For the past couple of years, my classes have been senior level. The upperclassmen just don't have that same enthusiasm as the young ones who are just starting out."

"This is the best age. They haven't become cynical yet," he said with a good-natured chuckle. He tilted his head slightly, a thoughtful gleam in his eyes. "I can appreciate your teaching style. You do more than just lecture — you tell a story in a way that captures the imagination and lures them in. Brimley is lucky to have you, Tamryn."

"Thank you," she said with genuine gratitude. His praise was a balm to her tattered confidence. The recent developments within the department at Brimley had her feeling like the redheaded stepchild with pockmarks. She needed to hear that she was good at her job.

"I've been mulling over the Indigenous Women's Studies course ever since you mentioned it," Ezekiel continued. "Female students outnumber males two to one. I think it's something that would garner much interest from the students here."

"It's a fascinating and much understudied field," she said. "If I had more time, or assurances from the higher-ups at Brimley that they would support it, I would develop the course more fully."

"You don't think they would be interested in adding to the curriculum?"

Tamryn gave him a hapless shrug as she took another sip of coffee.

Actually, she was almost certain that they would add the course to the curriculum. She just didn't think she would be there to teach it.

She returned to the table in the archives room that had become like a second home over the weeks she'd been in Louisiana. But as she tried to concentrate on the information found within the tomes, Tamryn couldn't shake the uneasy feeling that had settled in her stomach.

What did she really want to gain from all of this?

She had set out on this journey with single-minded determination, her goal clearly spelled out. But during the course of a simple sophomore history class, her world had undergone a seismic shift.

She wanted to return to what she'd first loved about her job. She wanted to fulfill the promise she'd made to herself the day she learned that her doctoral dissertation had been accepted: that she would spend her life molding young minds and instilling in them a love for history.

She could argue that she was still doing that with the work she conducted while co-

cooned within the walls of this library, but Tamryn knew it wasn't the same. She needed to be hands-on. She needed to see the wonder in her students' eyes as she opened their world to the history surrounding them.

She needed to follow her heart back to what she truly loved.

A broad smile broke out across Matt's face as he drove up to Belle Maison and spotted Tamryn lounging on the wooden porch swing. He parked next to a van that was shrink-wrapped with the logo for a local swamp-tour company. He walked over to where she sat with one leg up, her foot planted on the slated swing.

Matt folded his arms over his chest as he leaned against an ornately carved porch column. "Looking pretty busy there."

"And you're looking mighty gleeful," she returned, setting her iPad on top of the notebook on the table next to her. "What's with that smile? Did Patrick Carter wind up in a coma this morning?"

Matt grinned. "I'm not that lucky."

"Just as well. You wouldn't want to win that seat by default."

"I'll take that win any way I can get it," he said, wringing a laugh from her. He pointed to the electronic tablet. "Find anything interesting?"

"Just the opposite," she said with a sigh. She picked up the iPad and swiped her finger across the touch screen. Then she turned it so that it faced him. There was a colorful chart with various offshoots extending from it.

"This is a timeline I created from the significant events I've been able to uncover about my grandmother's past. Do you see this big gray area? That's when the school was created. I just can't find anything linking her to it."

"What about Nicolette Gauthier? You said you believed she played a part in it."

She nodded, picking up the notebook and flipping through a few pages. "I was able to find a couple of articles from several newspapers that mentioned her support for the school, but none of them indicate her involvement in actually creating it. They just say that she and Micah were both strong supporters once the school opened."

Matt blew out an uneasy breath. "Look, Tamryn. I don't want to throw a wet blanket on all the work you've done. I know you've put years into this, but . . ."

"But?" she asked.

Before the words even came out of his

mouth, Matt had already decided that he could never hate himself as much as he did right now.

"Did you ever think that if the evidence is so hard to find, maybe there isn't any?"

The dejected look that traced across her features made the impossible possible — he actually hated himself even more than he had just a second ago.

"If I had a dollar for every time a colleague or well-meaning friend told me that, I could buy that huge mansion you live in," she said. "But I can't shake the feeling that's in here, Matt." She flattened her palm against her stomach. "Or here," she said, moving her hand up and covering her heart. "I can't explain it, but I know the evidence is there somewhere. I can't stop until I find it."

Matt blew out a breath. "Is there any way I can convince you to stop for at least tonight?" he asked.

She started to shake her head. "I have so much work to catch up on."

"You don't want to turn down this opportunity," he said. "Trust me."

"I don't doubt that whatever you have planned is spectacular, but —"

"You're going to tour Rosemead," Matt said.

She stopped short and stared up at him. "What?" she said in a barely audible whisper.

Matt pushed away from the column he'd been leaning on and went over to her. He crouched down until he was level with her face. "I decided to put some of my clout as a Gauthier to good use and called in a couple of favors."

"But Rosemead isn't open to the public. It isn't even occupied. I thought the owner lived somewhere in France."

"She does, but the curator lives here in Louisiana. She contacted the owner on my behalf, who granted her permission to give us a private tour. You're going to see the plantation where your great-great-great-grandmother worked as a slave."

The instant tears that sprang to her eyes did little to assuage the massive guilt Matt still felt over keeping the diary from her, but knowing that he could give her something that meant so much to her alleviated a small portion of his self-disgust. He followed Tamryn into the Victorian and sat on the bed and watched while she packed an overnight bag.

Twenty minutes later, they were heading west on Highway 190 toward what was known as the Florida Parishes. The area, located just east of Baton Rouge, was home to a number of former sugar and cotton plantation homes. Rosemead, the one Tamryn had mention while they lay in bed one evening, was the place where her ancestor had been born and worked as a slave until she was seventeen.

"I can hardly keep still," Tamryn said. She held her arm out. "And the goose bumps are back."

Matt looked over to find her fidgeting in the passenger seat. He reached over and grabbed her hand, rubbing his thumb back and forth over her smooth skin.

"Thank you for tonight," she said.

"We haven't even gotten there yet," Matt pointed out.

"I don't care. I know this will be one of the most unbelievable moments of my entire life. It's something I've dreamed about since I first started researching Adeline West's past. I truly cannot think of a single thing you could have done that could mean more to me than this."

Matt could. He could turn this car around, drive to the Gauthier Mansion and hand her the leather-bound diary hidden in that safe.

He brought her hand to his lips and kissed the back of it. They continued the drive in relative quiet, with Tamryn making a few comments here and there about sights they passed. When they pulled up to the closed gates of the Rosemead Plantation, Matt spotted a white SUV parked on the other side of it. A slim woman with a thick silver braid draped over her left shoulder walked up to the gate and opened one side. She waved them in.

Matt drove through and stopped a couple of yards inside the gate. The curator came up to his car and leaned forward to speak into the window he'd just lowered. "Continue on to the house. I'll be there in a few minutes."

By the time they parked in front of the large, two-story, French Creole–style house, Matt could practically feel the excitement emanating from Tamryn.

"Will you be able to hold it together?" he asked her.

She shook her head. "Not a chance in hell."

He chuckled as they exited the car. The curator pulled up next to his car, introduced herself as Peggy Dauphine and started them on their private tour.

Matt held himself a few feet back as the curator pointed out the classic architecture and features unique to Rosemead. They toured nearly every room of the huge house and several of the surrounding buildings on the grounds.

They approached the small rectangular structures toward the back of the property. Tamryn's steps slowed. As she studied the tiny buildings crudely constructed out of centuries-old mud bricks, Matt studied her. Her fingers trembled as she raised them to her mouth, and a small gasp escaped her lips.

Matt was quickly at her side. He captured her upper arms and gave them a squeeze.

"It's okay if you lose it," he whispered into her ear.

"I won't," she said, shaking her head slightly. "It's just . . . this is where she was born. The slave quarters at Rosemead is where Adeline and her brother Adler were both born. It's where her father, my great-great-great-great-grandfather, is buried."

She turned to him. "It's so much to process, Matt. I'm not sure if I even can."

Matt took her into his arms and held on for untold moments. He looked over Tamryn's shoulders to find Peggy smiling, tears glistening in her own eyes.

They spent another half hour walking the grounds of Rosemead. Despite orders from the home's owner that photographs were not to be taken, Peggy allowed Tamryn to snap several shots of various structures.

As they drove out of the gate and back onto the road, Matt once again took Tamryn's hand in his. He craved physical contact with her at all times.

"I will never be able to thank you enough," she whispered.

"You don't have to thank me at all," Matt said. "You have no idea how much it meant to me to be able to do that for you."

She looked over at him, gratitude and what Matt could only describe as love on her face.

"You are such a good man."

Her words caused his stomach to turn in on itself. "Don't give me more credit than I deserve," Matt said. "All I did was call in a couple of favors."

"But you did that for me when you didn't have to."

"I wanted to." He kissed the back of her fingers. "And the night isn't over." He released her hand just long enough to flip on his turn signal.

"What's this?" Tamryn asked as they pulled up to The Guesthouse at Hemingbough.

"This is where you put aside all of the worries over your job and your research, and you allow yourself to be pampered."

"Oh, Matthew," she whispered.

Matt leaned over the center console and pressed his lips to hers. "I don't want you to worry about anything tonight. I just want you to enjoy. Can you do that for me?"

A tremulous smile drew across her lips. "I don't think that will be very hard."

Tamryn reclined on the silk-covered chaise, sipping the champagne Matt had handed her before he began the decadent foot rub she was now being treated to.

"Do you know I have never had anyone rub my feet before?" she said.

He looked up at her, his grin positively sinful. "I have an ulterior motive." Tamryn crooked a curious brow. "As much as I'm enjoying rubbing your feet, there are other parts of your body that I've been dying to touch all day."

With a wicked smile, she set her champagne glass on the side table and reached for him, pulling him on top of her. "You do not have to butter me up with foot rubs in order to get that," she said.

Matt leaned in and captured her lips. He then made quick work of relieving her of her clothes, getting them both naked in record time. He switched their positions, sliding underneath her and fitting her on top of him so that she straddled his lap. Tamryn braced her hands on his chest as with one hand he held her waist while he used the other to guide his rigid erection inside her.

Their twin groans of pleasure rent the air. She moved her body up and down his length, her head pitched back in ecstasy as she relished the feel of the silky, rock-hard flesh invading her body. She pumped her hips, increasing the pace until she was driving up and down in rapid succession.

Tamryn's body erupted, her world shattering as her orgasm hit swift and hard. She fell forward, resting her head against Matt's chest.

He ran a damp palm down her back before cradling the back of her head in his hand. He used his other hand to lift her chin. His eyes filled with hot promise, he whispered, "I'm not done with you."

A shudder coursed through her bloodstream at the seductive tone she heard in his voice.

Matt slipped from underneath her and carried her to the bed. Tamryn's limbs were still so weak from the aftershocks of her first orgasm that moving was practically impossible.

With Matt, that wasn't an issue.

He climbed onto the bed and spread her legs wide. He gave no warning at all before he dived for her center, his tongue lashing at her heated flesh. He flattened his palms against her inner thighs and pushed her legs wider, giving him unencumbered access to the very heart of her.

Tamryn pitched her head back, thrusting her hips forward to meet his skillful mouth. Sensation shimmered along her skin as he drove his tongue inside her, over and over and over again.

The familiar quake started low in her belly, but the buildup wasn't slow this time. This time she came hard and fast, her legs shaking with the force of her release.

Tamryn collapsed back onto the bed. She couldn't move, could barely think.

The only thought that managed to make it past the sensual haze surrounding her was the difficulty she would face when it was time to leave this man. Of all the things she'd ever done in her life, saying goodbye to Matt would be the hardest.

CHAPTER 11

Matt pulled up to the two-story home on Camp Street in New Orleans's historic Garden District. Grabbing his laptop from the front passenger seat, he jumped out of his car and slammed the door shut. As he marched up the walkway, Matt realized that he could count on one hand how many times he'd been here in the five years since his father bought this home. It was five times more than he'd wanted to darken this doorstep.

The front door opened before Matt had a chance to knock on it.

"Hello, Matthew," Marion Samuels answered. Matt stared at his family's former housekeeper, not surprised to see her standing here.

"Where is he?" Matt bit out.

"He's in his office," she said, moving out of the way so that Matt could pass.

He refused to allow her being there to affect him. He no longer cared what his father did with his own life. It was when he stuck his nose into Matt's business that they had a problem.

He bounded up the stairs and headed straight for the rear of the house, toward his father's home office. He didn't even give him the courtesy of knocking; it wasn't as if his father would understand courtesy anyway. Matt walked into the large office and spotted his father through the French doors, sitting out on the balcony with his leg crossed and a newspaper opened in his lap.

Matt went to him and set the laptop on the small, round iron table next to his father's chair. The only other thing on the table was an ashtray that held a smoldering cigarette.

Matt braced his feet apart and folded his hands over his chest. "What in the hell do you think you're doing?" he asked.

"Don't start this with me, Matthew."

Leroy picked up the cigarette and took a long drag on it. Matt had to fight the urge to slap it out of his hands. The only reason he didn't was out of respect for his mother, who had demanded Matt show this bastard some respect, despite the fact that he hadn't earned a damn bit of it.

His father gestured to the laptop. "If you

brought that to show me the commercial, it's not necessary. I already saw it and approved it."

"I didn't," Matt said. "Even though there's a voice that sounds remarkably like mine at the end of the commercial saying that I do. Whose voice is it anyway?"

"A voice actor. He's pretty good, isn't he?"

"I could have you arrested," Matt spat.

"Stop being so dramatic," Leroy said. He pointed to the fabric-covered chair on the other side of the table. "Sit down. We need to go through the strategy for the last half of this campaign. The polling I had done shows that you're only two points ahead of Carter. That's within the margin of error."

Matt huffed out a laugh and shook his head. "You're too damn smart to be this dense, so I guess it's just cockiness." He leaned forward until he was only inches from his father's face. "What makes you think I would take campaign advice from you? What makes you think I would take *any* kind of advice from you? Do you think I look at you and see someone I want to mimic my life after? A man who left his dying wife's hospital room so he could go home and screw his housekeeper? A man who's taken so much in bribe money that he owes more favors than he will ever be able to fulfill?"

"And your hands are so clean?"

"They're a hell of a lot cleaner than yours are."

"Really?" His brows peaked. "So all those phone calls and lunches you had with Lyle Peterson of the Lakeline Group were just, what, you being courteous? Welcoming them to the neighborhood?

"But wait," Leroy continued. "You're the one who brought them to the neighborhood, aren't you? I think I remember Lyle telling me that when we had dinner."

The smug smile on the bastard's face was just begging to be knocked off. "To say you loathe me so damn much, it looks like you still learned how to conduct business like your old man," he said.

"Don't you ever compare me to you," Matt snarled. "I didn't take a single dime from those developers. I was trying to help the people of Gauthier. I wasn't trying to help myself like you would."

"So why is it still such a big secret, Matt? Why haven't you gone up and down Main Street and told each one of those business owners that you're the reason they nearly lost their livelihoods?"

His father picked up the cigarette and took another long pull on it. "You can hate me all you want to, but you're still a Gauthier. You've still got that blood running through your veins. The tragedy here is that you've got so much damn potential. If you didn't have so much of your mother in you, I could —"

Matt grabbed a handful of the collar on his father's robe and pulled him up to his face. "That's the last time you mention her in my presence, especially when you have that woman living here."

His father's eyes darted between Matt's face and where he clutched the robe. Matt let go of the collar and took a step back.

"You already cost Ben his job by conning him into doing that commercial. I fired him this morning." He pointed a finger at his father's face. "Stay the hell away from my campaign."

Without another word Matt walked back out the way he came. He passed Marion on his way out the door, but didn't take the time to acknowledge her. He could go the rest of his life without ever seeing either of them again.

As he drove the few miles to the Civil District Court Building on Loyola Avenue in downtown New Orleans, Matt tried to block out the confrontation so that he could mentally prepare for the hearing on Mrs.

Black's case, but his father's words continued to reverberate in his head.

Was he turning out to be just like Leroy Gauthier?

Every lie he told, every secret he harbored, they all helped to mold him in his father's likeness, and the thought made Matt sick. He had no choice. He had to come clean about all of it. Matt wasn't sure how much longer he could live with himself if he didn't.

"Oh, my God."

Tamryn clutched the edges of the table she'd occupied for the past five hours in the bowels of Tulane University's renowned archives room. Her skin tingled. Her breathing escalated. Her entire being buzzed with the mixture of excitement and disbelief cluttering her brain as she stared at the flyer, encased in archival laminate and sitting inconspicuously in a binder.

"Oh, my God," she breathed again. Her hand shook as she ran her finger across the plastic, the words swimming before her as her eyes filled with tears.

Negro School to Open.

Below the headline was a picture of her great-great-great-grandmother and Nicolette Gauthier. It was a staged shot with the two of them holding up textbooks. The short, two-paragraph article below stated that, despite strong opposition, the classes in reading and arithmetic would be taught to both slave children and free blacks. Tamryn swiped at the tears of relief that flowed down her cheeks.

After all the years of searching, after all the roadblocks — doubts from colleagues, doubts in herself — finally, *finally* she'd found proof. It wasn't the diary that Tamryn knew was out there somewhere, but it was enough to prove that Adeline West had changed history.

After she'd calmed down enough to stop her body from shaking, Tamryn went to the librarian, requesting copies of what she had found. While the man made copies of the items that weren't too sensitive to be reproduced, Tamryn packed up the rest of her research materials.

Once she had the documented proof safely put away in her computer bag, she left the library, her body still humming with energy. She couldn't wait the few minutes it would take to get to her car before she called Matt. She sat on a stone bench under a towering oak tree and dialed his number.

She didn't give him a chance to speak after his initial "Hello."

"Matt," she practically screamed. She

wasn't sure her skin would be able to contain all the excitement flooding her veins. "I found it! I found proof of the school Adeline West and Nicolette Gauthier opened together!"

The complete silence that met her on the other end of the line had Tamryn's head rearing back. She looked at the phone, wondering if the call had dropped.

"Matt?"

"Yeah. Yeah, I'm here," he said. "Can I call you back? I'm heading into court."

"Um, sure," Tamryn said, ignoring the tremor of unease that traveled down her spine. "I'll, uh, talk to you later."

On her way back to Gauthier, she called Victoria, needing to share her news with somebody. This was too monumental to keep bottled up inside. She was relieved when Victoria answered the phone and expressed nearly as much enthusiasm as Tamryn had. They talked so long that Tamryn had to remind Victoria that she had a class of students waiting.

She ended the call, smiling at the excitement she'd heard in her coworker's voice. Maybe it was something only a fellow history buff could get excited about.

But Matt knew how important this was to her. He knew how hard she had been working to find this missing link to her grand-mother's past.

"He was going into court," Tamryn reminded herself. What had she expected him to do? Drop everything and run to her side so they could pop open a bottle of champagne?

Tamryn drove to Belle Maison so that she could shower and change into one of her more comfortable sundresses. She found Phylicia and Mya out under the gazebo, enjoying iced tea. Both women were thrilled about the document Tamryn had found. Mya called her husband, who in addition to coaching the baseball team also taught American history at the high school.

If Matt had exhibited even a tenth of the enthusiasm Corey Anderson did, Tamryn surmised that she wouldn't have the uncomfortable feeling in her gut that she hadn't been able to shake since her abbreviated call with Matt.

She left Phylicia and Mya outside and went up to her room, dillydallying around for another two hours before, finally, she couldn't take it anymore. She headed for the Gauthier mansion, hoping she'd given Matt enough time to get home.

Her shoulders drooped in relief when she drove around the back of the house and spotted his car parked in its usual spot under the portico just off the entrance to the kitchen. Tamryn gave two sharp taps on the door, and seconds later, Matt opened it.

"Hi," she answered with a smile she couldn't contain.

"Hello," he said.

His subdued expression caught her off guard. He walked over to the kitchen island, where a highball glass filled halfway with amber liquid sat next to a parcel of mail.

Tamryn's steps slowed as she rounded the kitchen island. "Are you okay, Matt?"

He nodded. "You?"

"I'm more than okay. I'm perfect." That smile was back again, bigger than ever. She'd smiled so much this afternoon her cheeks hurt. "I found it," she said. "I found proof that Adeline West and Nicolette Gauthier opened a school for free blacks and slave children."

Tamryn wasn't sure what she expected, but it was definitely not the apathetic nod he gave her. "Matt, did you hear what I said? I found my proof."

He took a sip of his whiskey, then he put the glass down and reached for her hands. "I'm happy for you," he said. "I know how much this means for your career, and for you personally."

Disquiet slithered down Tamryn's spine. She cleared her throat before she spoke. "Call me crazy, but it doesn't sound as if you're all that happy for me. I'm not really sure what's going on, but —"

"Come with me," Matt said, but then he stopped, holding up a finger. "Wait one minute." He picked up the glass and drained the rest of the whiskey. "There. That's better."

The uneasy feeling traveling through her intensified. She had never seen him this way before.

"Matt, is something wrong?" she asked.

"Yes." He huffed out a humorless laugh, shaking his head. "Something has been wrong for a very long time."

He wrapped his fingers around her wrist and gently urged her to follow him.

They walked to the family library on the left side of the house. Tamryn had only been in the room once, during her first visit to the mansion. She stood just beyond the threshold of the door while Matt walked over to a portrait of Micah Gauthier. He grasped the gilded frame and unhooked the portrait from the wall, revealing a safe.

As he turned the knob on the combination lock, Tamryn noticed that his fingers were shaking.

"Matt, what are you doing?"

His chin dropped to his chest as he braced his left hand on the wall. "Coming clean," he said.

He opened the safe and rifled around inside for a moment. She couldn't tell what he retrieved, but her blood pulsed with a mixture of excitement and dread in anticipation of it. When he turned, Tamryn's stomach dropped at the sight of the worn, leather-bound book.

She couldn't move. Her feet remained rooted in that spot, her eyes zeroed in on the book in Matt's hands as he closed the distance between them.

"It wasn't just the stuff of legends," he said. He held the book out to her. "My aunt Nicolette's diary."

Trembling fingers floated up to Tamryn's lips. She looked at the journal, then at Matt.

"But . . ." she started, but she didn't have words. She didn't have anything.

Except for hurt. Suddenly, she had all the hurt she could handle and more.

"This . . . this whole time?" Tamryn choked out. "You've had this the whole time?"

A small part of her hoped that he would say that he'd just found out from a long-lost family member about the hidden safe at the Gauthier mansion, but Tamryn knew she was grasping at straws. The guilt that washed over Matt's face was all the answer she needed.

"How could you?" she whispered.

His throat moved as he swallowed, but he remained silent.

"How. Could. You?" she asked again with enough force to shake the walls. "Is everything in there?" Tamryn asked, pointing at the diary she hadn't summoned the courage to touch just yet. "The school? The connection to Adeline?"

He nodded. And her heart broke in two.

"My God, Matt. You knew how much this meant to my career. You knew what this meant to *me.*"

"I'm sorry," he said.

"Sorry?" She took a step back. "You think *sorry* is enough?"

"I couldn't share it with you."

"Why not?"

"Because there's a lot more in here than just the information about your grandmother and Nicolette's school. There's . . . everything. Everything about my family and what they've done. Everything about how the Gauthiers lied and cheated their way into owning this town, how Micah and Nicolette's son nearly burned half the buildings on Main Street to the ground and how they covered up the death of the man who died in the fire."

A chill traveled down Tamryn's spine, but she shook it off. Whatever had happened, it had happened a long time ago.

"What does any of that have to do with my research?" she asked.

"Everything," he said. "You've been calling since last summer, trying to dig up these skeletons. I couldn't let you do that. There was too much at stake."

"Like my career?"

"Like *my* career!" he said. "Do you know what Patrick Carter will do to me if this gets out?"

"Patrick Carter can't use what your ancestors did nearly two hundred years ago to hurt your campaign, Matt."

"No, but he can use what my father did and what his father did. He can use what *I* did. This diary is just the start, Tamryn. It's the first item in a long line of evidence that shows that the Gauthier family has been nothing but a cancer to this town since the day it was founded."

Tamryn shook her head. "It's not an excuse," she said. "You let me search for weeks, killing myself in that library for hours every day. You listened to me lament about how hard this research was, and question whether or not I was wasting my time looking for something that didn't exist. And this entire time, you knew it did!"

He pinched his eyes shut and threw his head back. The pain etched across his face meant nothing to her, not when she was feeling so much of her own pain.

Matt held the diary out to her. "Take it," he said. "I don't care anymore. Just take it."

Tamryn almost turned around and walked out without it, just to spite him. But her career was worth a hell of a lot more to her than the brief satisfaction she would get from hurting Matt. She took the diary from his fingers, turned and strode out of the library, never once looking back.

When Tamryn arrived at Belle Maison, she climbed onto the bed. Handling the diary with supreme care, she laid it on a pillow and gingerly opened the brittle pages. She sat with her head hunched over the diary for more than an hour, poring over stories about the perils Adeline and Nicolette faced during the early stages of the school's development. Twice the small shed they'd used as a schoolroom was burned to the ground. Both had suffered numerous threats to their lives, but had soldiered on.

Tamryn swiped at the tears that continued

to stream down her cheeks. Whether they were tears of pride or tears of relief, she couldn't be sure. She'd searched so long, and to finally have this proof of her great-great-great-grandmother's tireless efforts to educate young children of color . . . it was overwhelming.

That was what she was. She was over-whelmed with pride.

Her phone rang, and Tamryn was sur-prised that she was able to tear herself away from the pages of the diary long enough to check it. A small part of her thought — hoped — that it was Matt calling to apolo-gize. It would take a lot to rectify the pain he'd caused her, but now that she'd had some time to come to grips with her emo-tions, she would be more receptive to an apology than she had been just a few hours ago.

But it wasn't Matt on the other end of the line; it was Victoria. Tamryn felt the blood drain from her face as she listened to her colleague. When she ended the call, she quickly pulled up a travel website and booked the first flight back to Boston.

CHAPTER 12

Matt wasn't even thinking as he got in his car and started for Belle Maison. He just knew he needed to get there. He needed to get to Tamryn. Before he did anything else, he needed to explain to her why he'd deliberately kept the diary from her.

But he'd done that already. There wasn't much more he could add to the reasons he'd given her before she'd stormed out of his family's library.

He'd kept the thing she'd spent years searching for from her to save his own ass, even though he knew how much it meant to her. Maybe if he'd asked her to keep the other stories hidden within the pages of the diary a secret, she would have honored his request. He hadn't given her the chance.

Matt briefly shut his eyes. He was so overwhelmed with self-disgust he could hardly stand to be around himself.

He pulled up to Belle Maison and climbed

out of the car, taking the four porch steps in two strides. He knocked once before opening the door he knew Phil kept unlocked most of the day. He bounded up the stairs, but Phylicia's yell stopped him halfway to the top.

"Hey, where are you going?" she called from the base of the stairs. She had a dish towel slung over her shoulder and a juice glass in her hand.

"I need to talk to Tamryn," Matt said.

"She isn't here," Phil answered.

Her words sucked all the wind from his sails. Matt trudged down the stairs and stopped in front of Phil. "Where is she?"

"I'm not sure I should say anything. It would be bad business practice."

Matt eyed her. "Don't do that to me, Phil. I need to know where she is."

"She went to Boston."

Matt's chest felt as if it was caving in. "Boston?" he choked out.

"About an hour ago. She left most of her things, so she'll be back."

"Did she say how long she would be gone?"

She shook her head. "Sorry."

Matt dragged both hands down his face.

"You messed up, didn't you?" Phil asked.

"More than I've ever messed up before,"

he admitted.

"Well, you probably have a few days to figure out a way to make up for it. I suggest you start working on it right now." Phil patted him on the arm and headed toward the back of the Victorian, where the kitchen was located.

Having no reason to linger at Belle Maison, Matt got into his car and started back toward his house. He took the scenic route home, driving through downtown Gauthier, past Heritage Park and his law firm. As he meandered through the residential neighborhood south of Main Street, Matt thought about all the chances he'd had to tell Tamryn about the diary. He should have trusted her with the information.

But he'd chosen to lie instead. Even though he knew how much it would hurt her. Even though he knew how much that diary had meant to her. He'd deliberately kept it from her. He felt like the world's worst bastard.

The deception reminded him too much of his father. So much that Matt could feel the nausea building in his belly.

The thought of being no better than Leroy Gauthier was enough to suffocate him. He would give anything not to turn out like the man who'd fathered him.

Even if it meant giving up his shot at the state senate.

A sharp ache pierced his chest, but Matt did his best to ignore it.

If that was the price he had to pay for the sins he'd committed against this town, against the woman he'd grown to love, then he would pay it. It was only fair after what he'd done.

Tamryn stopped just before the thick wooden doors that led to the History Department's suite of offices in McNamara Hall on the small, elegant campus of Brimley College. She pulled in a deep breath, trying to get her chaotic emotions under control.

She wasn't even sure what she should be feeling right now: anger, fear, disappointment? They were all swirling around in her gut.

When Victoria called to tell her about rumors she'd heard circulating around campus, it had put Tamryn on edge. But ever since reading the email Reid had sent late last night, letting her know that her position at Brimley was being vacated, Tamryn's emotions had run the gamut. The fact that the bastard hadn't had the courtesy to call her to tell her she was being let go had spurred her strongest feeling. Rage.

There was a special meeting today between several members of the Board of Regents, the dean and the History Department chair. She had not been invited, but Tamryn refused to go down without a fight, especially now that she had the proof she needed to complete the book about Adeline West. But before she met with Brimley's powers that be, she and Reid had business they needed to settle.

After another deep, calming, mind-clearing breath, Tamryn walked through the History Department's double doors. She was greeted by the receptionist, Lydia, who waved to her while she spoke directions to McNamara Hall into the phone. For a moment, Tamryn wondered if she was giving directions to whomever had been hired to replace her.

Tamryn bypassed her office — which she vowed would *remain* her office — and headed down the hallway to the room at the very end of the suite. It was the office that every professor aspired to one day occupy. The fact that Reid Hayes now occupied it made Tamryn's lip curl in distaste.

She applauded herself for knocking like a civilized human being when she got to the door, when what she really wanted to do was tear into the office and run her fingernails down his face. Reid's laconic voice called for her to enter. When she did, he looked up and a sarcastic smile surfaced on his lips.

"A simple reply to my email would have sufficed, Tamryn. You didn't have to fly all the way here just to say goodbye."

"If you think I'm giving up my job without a fight, you must be out of your mind. I know why you're doing this," she said.

"Hmm . . ." He leaned back in his chair and tapped his ink pen against his lips. "Could it be because your classes barely hit the minimum number of students required to maintain eligibility, or is it because you've spent years doing research that's led to nowhere?"

"You mean after the year I spent conducting your research without getting any credit for it?"

"We never discussed you being coauthor," he said. "You're the one who made assumptions you shouldn't have made."

"You are such a bastard."

He stretched his hands out. "And look what being a bastard got me. Not bad."

Tamryn stared at the man she'd spent nearly two years of her life with. The thought of sleeping with him made her stomach turn. The thought of working with him in any capacity whatsoever sickened her even more. Why was she fighting for a job that would put her in close proximity to this asshole?

Tamryn thought about Ezekiel Marsh and how enthusiastic he was about her research. She knew she had a job waiting for her in Louisiana if she wanted one. And if Zeke wasn't ready to hire her just yet, she could take the time off to finally finish her grandmother's book.

She didn't need Brimley, and she sure as hell didn't need to grovel at Reid's feet. The diary tucked away in the drawer of the chest back at Belle Maison had opened up a whole new world for her.

"You know what, Reid? I flew to Boston to fight for my job, but you just reminded me of why I would be crazy to come back here. I don't need this. Now that I have proof that Adeline West started the first school for slave children —"

"Proof?" Reid cut her off, sitting up straight in his chair.

"Yes," Tamryn said, unable to stop the smug smile that drew across her face. "Remember that diary that you told me was just an old family legend? I have it. I've touched it. And I've read everything that

269

Nicolette Fortier Gauthier wrote regarding the school that she and Adeline West started.

"I don't need you, Reid. And despite what you think, I never did. I am an amazing teacher who comes from a long line of amazing teachers. However, to show that there are no hard feelings, when my book is published and I'm on the speaker circuit, I'll give Brimley a nice discount when you bring me in to give a lecture on my book."

Tamryn gave him a saccharine smile and walked out of the office.

She stopped at Lydia's desk on her way out of the suite of offices. The receptionist looked at her with pity in her eyes.

"Hello, Dr. West. I'm sorry," she said.

"I'm not," Tamryn said. The realization that she wasn't sorry, that she was, in fact, ecstatic, caused a huge smile to break out across her face. "I don't have much in my office. Can you see that my things are boxed up and delivered to my condo? I need to get back down to Louisiana and just don't have time to waste clearing things out at Brimley."

"I will," Lydia said with a hint of awe in her voice. "You look amazing, Dr. West. Happy."

"I am," Tamryn said. "I can't remember when I've been happier." She smiled again.

"I'll make sure I stop back in a couple of weeks when I return to pack up my condo."

"You're leaving Boston altogether?"

Tamryn nodded.

"But I thought they just made the decision to let you go yesterday," Lydia said.

"Yeah, but I think I made the decision to let them go a while ago. I just hadn't realized it."

She gave Lydia a little goodbye wave and walked out of the History Department, feeling freer than she had in her entire life.

Matt stood against the wall of the back room of Morning Star Baptist Church's fellowship hall in Maplesville, his eyes closed, his heart beating like a drum against the walls of his chest. He was resolved in what he had to do, but it still made him ill. He would give anything not to give up his run for state senate, but he was done with the deceit. Not just his own, but of the entire Gauthier family.

It was time for people to learn the truth.

He only wished that Tamryn was here to witness him coming clean. He hadn't spoken to her since she'd left him standing in the library at the Gauthier mansion two nights ago. His calls had gone unanswered; so had his dozen text messages.

"Hey, man, you ready for this?" Matt opened his eyes and found Mason Coleman, his friend and fellow attorney from Maplesville, walking toward him.

"I'm ready," Matt answered.

He followed Mason, stopping at the edge of the door that led from the back room. The front area of the hall was set up with two stools on either side of a desk. This town hall–style debate was the final event between him and Patrick Carter before the special election in two weeks.

It ate at Matt's gut that he'd come so close. This area deserved better than Patrick Carter as their state senator. It deserved better than him, too.

The pastor of Morning Star Baptist Church, who was sponsoring this final debate, called for a moment of prayer before the start of the event. After that was done, Matt and Patrick Carter were called to the floor, entering from different sides. Both took their seats, but after one final mental check that he was ready to do this, Matt stood and walked over to Pastor Ryland.

"If I could, I would like to have a couple of minutes to address the audience," Matt said. Carter started to bluster, but Matt stopped him with a hand. "You'll want to hear this."

He turned to the crowd, which was at least 80 percent Gauthier residents, despite the fact that the debate was being held in Maplesville. Matt let out a deep breath and began.

"The people of Gauthier have always been extremely good to my family, but it pains me to admit that it hasn't always been reciprocated. Since the fire of 1882 that nearly burned down the town, the Gauthiers have been wreaking havoc on this area." Matt took in the confused faces in the crowd. "For years stories have been told about Micah Gauthier helping to rescue the Callis family from the fire and saving other lives, but the part that never gets told is that it was Micah's son who started the fire."

Low murmurs started to spread through the room.

"This is just one instance in a long line of transgressions of the Gauthier family. The water-treatment plant that was built didn't go to the best company for the job — it went to the company that was willing to line my grandfather's pockets while he was mayor of Gauthier.

"And the outlet mall here in Maplesville . . ." Matt paused. He had to swallow twice before he could speak again. "I'm the reason it's here."

A collective gasp echoed over the crowd.

"Matthew Gauthier, what are you talking about?" It was Eloise Dubois, who'd stood up from her seat.

"I'm the one who brought the Lakeline Group to this area," Matt admitted. "At the time, I thought the outlet mall would be a boost to Gauthier's economy. I had no idea the company would choose to build in Maplesville instead. I had no idea *any* of this would happen, but it did."

Matt closed his eyes for a moment before continuing, "I am ending my candidacy for state senate."

This time, the gasp that tore through the crowd was so loud that he felt it on his skin. "I'm not the man you all thought I was," he continued. "I'm not the right man to represent District Twelve."

"Are you the same man who gave five thousand dollars in scholarship money to the local high school?"

Matt's head popped up. He looked toward the back of the room and saw Tamryn walking up the center aisle.

"That outlet mall has cost me a lot of business," Nathan Robottom chimed in.

Tamryn turned to him. "Didn't you tell me just last week that Matt helped your hardware store get on the list of approved suppliers for the new concrete plant that's about to start construction on Highway 190?" she asked.

"I guess you're right," Nathan muttered.

Tamryn continued her journey up the aisle. "Are you the same man who organized the all-night read-in event to kick off a mentorship program?" she asked Matt.

"And the 5K," Mya Dubois-Anderson added from the second row.

"And the Thanksgiving food drive," Mariska Thomas, of all people, stood up and said.

When Tamryn arrived at the front of the hall, she turned to face the crowd and pointed to Matt. "In the few weeks that I've spent here, I haven't seen anyone do more for the people of District Twelve than this man."

Murmurs of agreement reverberated around the room. In that moment, Matt realized just how much Gauthier had embraced her as one of their own. He stood there in disbelief, stunned and incredibly humbled as she spoke on his behalf.

He'd spent the past twenty-four hours preparing to end his candidacy and begin what he knew would be a long journey of gaining the forgiveness of fellow Gauthier residents. And an even longer journey of gaining Tamryn's forgiveness.

But here she was, like an apparition conjured by his imagination. Speaking on his behalf, standing up for him.

What in the world had he ever done to deserve someone like her in his life?

"We're not letting you quit," Eloise Dubois said. A majority of the crowd began to applaud.

"Now, wait a minute," Patrick Carter started.

Matt turned, a smile on his face. "I was mistaken," he said. "Looks like we have a debate to start."

He looked at Tamryn, who had a soft smile on her lips. *Good luck,* she mouthed.

He didn't need luck. Now that she was there, he had everything he needed.

Tamryn stood off to the side of the church hall, unable to wipe the grin from her face as she watched Matt completely annihilate Patrick Carter in their final town-hall debate. She still couldn't get over the fact that he had been about to drop out of the race. Was he crazy? Matt was so much more worthy than his opponent. Anyone who listened with even half an ear would know within minutes of hearing the two expound on what they would provide as members of the state senate that Matt was the better man.

He had the people of this area's best interests at heart. They would be fools not to elect him. Based on the raucous applause when he gave his final statement at the conclusion of the debate, Tamryn was pretty sure they would all have the chance to see just what type of state senator he would be.

The debate ended and Matt was immediately swarmed by residents from Gauthier. Several of the ladies from the civic association gave him hugs and kissed his cheek, their reassuring smiles warming Tamryn's heart. These people loved him, and for good reason. Matthew Gauthier's heart was pure gold.

She'd gone over the reasons he'd kept the diary hidden from her over and over these past two days, and Tamryn had come to realize what he was up against. For some reason, Matt had taken it upon himself to rectify what he saw as a lifetime's worth of transgressions by his family against the people of Gauthier. As misguided as he was, Tamryn now understood. She'd posed a threat to all the plans he'd had in place to make up for his family's past misdeeds. As much as she wanted to hold it against him, Tamryn knew she couldn't.

He finally came to stand before her. The myriad emotions on his face made her heart hurt.

"Thank you," he said.

"You're welcome. Although I didn't do anything."

"Except stop me from making the biggest mistake of my life?" he asked. "Make that the second biggest. The biggest mistake of my life was hurting you."

It was painful to pull in the deep breath she took. "Matt."

He took her hands in his. "Don't say anything. Let me first tell you how sorry I am."

"Matt, you don't have to."

"Yes, I do," he said. "I lied to you, willfully."

"Because you thought you were doing the right thing."

He shook his head. "Don't make excuses for me. I was trying to save my own ass. I knew how much that diary meant to you, and I still kept it from you. I will never be able to make up for that, even though I will try for the rest of my life. Even if it means flying to Boston every weekend to grovel at your feet."

"Unless you're going to see the changing of the leaves or a Red Sox game, you won't have much reason to go to Boston."

His forehead crinkled in confusion. "What are you saying?"

"I lost my position at Brimley," Tamryn said.

His eyes slowly shut. "If you'd had that proof for your research, you could have saved it, couldn't you? Dammit, Tamryn, I am so sorry."

"You shouldn't be," she said. "Now that I'm no longer at Brimley, I can take the position Ezekiel Marsh offered me yesterday when I called to tell him I'm available."

Matt's eyes popped open. Tamryn couldn't contain her smile.

"I won't be able to start until the spring semester, but that's actually perfect. It gives me time to find a place to live and to finally finish writing Adeline West's story."

"You have a place to live," he said. "If you think you're living anywhere but with me, you're crazy."

Matt pulled her into his arms and squeezed so tight Tamryn thought he would break her back.

"Oh, my God, I love you," he whispered against her ear.

"I love you, too, Senator."

Resounding applause and cheers sounded behind them. Tamryn burst out laughing as

279

she looked over Matt's shoulder and found a number of eyes on them.

"I hope you're prepared for life as a Gauthier in the town of Gauthier."

"You've done pretty well. I think I can handle it." She cradled his cheeks between her hands, urging his head down. Her lips hovering just inches from his, she whispered, "I cannot think of anything I'd rather be than a Gauthier."

EPILOGUE

Matt held up his cup of punch, joining in as Corey Anderson led a toast to his victory over Patrick Carter. It had been pretty certain from early on that he was going to win the senate seat, but Matt had decided not to accept his win until Carter called to concede. That call had come a few minutes ago.

"The people of District Twelve, and the entire town of Gauthier, are getting themselves a damn fine state senator, and we all could not be happier," Corey said. His words were followed by a roar of cheers and a call for Matt to give a speech.

He set his cup on the table and walked up to the podium that had been set up at the front of the room in the Masonic Lodge that he'd rented for his campaign-watch party. He'd opened it to the public, and of course, nearly all of Gauthier had turned out for the event.

"I'm not going to take up too much of your time. Everyone here already knows how I feel about them, and after tonight, I know how you feel about me, too."

"We love you, Matt!" someone called from the crowd.

"I love you, too," Matt said with a grin. "And I want to thank you all once again for your support, not just for tonight but throughout all of my years of practicing law in Gauthier. I vow to do everything within my power to live up to the potential you all apparently see in me. Thank you once again for electing me to represent this district in the Louisiana State Senate."

Matt accepted the applause, then left the podium. He headed straight for Tamryn.

"Very good, Senator. Short and sweet and, as always, full of charm."

"Happy I didn't disappoint."

"I don't think you could ever disappoint the people here."

"What about my future wife?" he asked, leaning in and giving her lips a swift kiss. "I want to make sure I don't disappoint her, either."

"I believe the only way you could do that is if you stopped falling asleep whenever I try to engage you in a discussion on history," she said.

He closed his eyes and let his head loll to the side, emitting a pretend snore. Tamryn pinched his arm. "Sorry." Matt shook his head and blinked rapidly. "You were saying something?"

"You are not funny."

"But you love me anyway, don't you?"

A smile tipped up the corners of her lips. "Yes, I do."

"Show me how much you love me, Professor."

She wrapped her arms around his neck. "Whatever you say, Senator."

ABOUT THE AUTHOR

Farrah Rochon had dreams of becoming a fashion designer as a teenager, until she discovered she would be expected to wear something other than jeans to work every day. Thankfully, the coffee shop where she writes does not have a dress code.

When Farrah is not penning stories, the avid sports fan feeds her addiction to football by attending New Orleans Saints games.